*Jerusalem plays hide and seek*

# Ariella Deem

# Jerusalem
## plays hide and seek

*translated with an afterword by Nelly Segal*

The Jewish Publication Society
Philadelphia · New York · Jerusalem
5747 · 1987

*Originally published in Hebrew under the title*
Yerushalayim Meśaḥeket Mahavo'im
*First published in 1976 by Trahlin, Inc., Tel Aviv*
*Second edition, 1982, by Ariel Publishers, Jerusalem*

*Translation copyright © 1987 by Nelly Segal, translator*
*First edition      All rights reserved*
*Manufactured in the United States of America*
*Library of Congress Cataloging in Publication Data*
Deem, Ariella.
  Jerusalem plays hide and seek.
  *Translation of: Yerushalayim meśaheket mahavo'im.*
  I. Title.
PJ5054.D55Y413   1987      892.4'36      86–27356
*ISBN 0–8276–0278–2*

DESIGN *Adrianne Onderdonk Dudden*

The city plays hide and seek among her names:
Yerushalaim, Al-Quds, Shalem, Jeru, Yeru, all the while
whispering her first Jebusite name
Y'vus, Y'vus, Y'vus, in the dark.

YEHUDA AMICHAI

# Translator's Note

My approach to this translation has been to render the stylistic originality that distinguishes Ariella Deem's writing as closely as the English will permit. I have tried to retain the archaic flavor of the language, the rhythmic and lyrical quality of the narrative. I have quoted from, and used the phraseology of, the King James Bible and the Soncino Talmud. I have not replaced unusual phrases with idiomatic expressions, nor have I clarified intended ambiguities. In the overall process of the translation, some omissions have been unavoidable, and Ariella, who was aware of these decisions, gave her approval.

The novella's subtitle, "*sippur b'shkufiot*" has been omitted from the English edition. One way of translating it would have been, "a tale of slides." But then, the Hebrew preposition "*b*" connotes more. It means *with,* as in "*with* an iron pen (*b'et*) and lead they were graven in to the rock for ever." And it also means *with and accompanied by,* as in "And all the women went out after her *with* timbrels (*b'tupim*) and dancing." *Jerusalem Plays Hide and Seek* is a tale of slides, told with slides and accompanied by them. I have not found an English equivalent for the preposition chosen by Ariella.

I would like to thank Prescott Evarts, Jr., of the English Department of Monmouth College, New Jersey, for his sensitive reading and insightful comments during the initial stage of this translation. Ariella's husband, Eddie Goldberg, has been with this book "ever since then." From its beginning. I am grateful to Eddie for calling my attention to the subtlest of Ariella's nuances, for his insistence on the correct spelling of names and places, and for his infinite faith and support throughout.

Nelly Segal

*Jerusalem plays hide and seek*

An autumn day in Boston lost its mind and masqueraded as spring. It was warm. The one in charge had raged throughout the night, and in the morning, the trees stood as if drenched by jugs full of paint. An oak tree, green only yesterday, stretched an entire yellow branch toward me. And the young sumac stuck out a wild, pink tongue. One tree had turned completely orange, then it was more—a deep purple with a single red branch soaring in the air.

I stepped out. Facing me, as usual, were the churchyard, the steeple, and the cross.

The sidewalk heat passed through my sandals, penetrated my feet, and flowed into my body. I brushed my hand over the hedges that surrounded the churchyard. The soft leaves swished against my fingers, and the sound was echoed by my sandals.

The street was deserted, except for the echo of my sandals. Had I shut my eyes for just a moment, I would have heard the piano tunes of the hour spill into the street. This was the hour when gently bred girls played their Chopin etudes to the street, through the closed shutters. They were surely dressed in neatly pressed clothes, the freshly mopped tile floors were still damp, and it was cool inside those rooms, beyond the closed shutters, beyond the hedges, beyond envy. Further along, over the treading of my sandals, the radios trilled in a velvety Yemenite voice: "I am athirst, I am a-a-a-thirst, for thy waters, for thy wa-a-a-ters, Jerusalem." On and on, to the Street of the Judges, on to the Street of the Prophets, through the square, westward—to the Mediterranean.

But here in Boston, west of me, lay not the Great Sea, but a large business street, at the end of which was an antique shop.

I went deep inside the store. A large globe, covered with dust, was couched among the pile of dark, heavy furniture. That huge black chair with the carvings—hadn't the Grand Inquisitor occupied it once? And the long copper telescope on the tripod—surely there was a time when inside the turrets, weary-eyed astronomers leaned against it. And the monastic, narrow wooden bench—many an apostate had paced around it in desperation.

What was I doing there among you, antiques? What had I to do with you? All I wanted was to walk down the street to the sea. To rent myself a lounge chair for thirty piastres. And a stool. Where Moishe the chair-keeper would bring me two slices of bread and margarine, topped with radish slices that were dotted with the tiny sparkling tear drops the salt had squeezed out of them. Then, after a while, Moishe would bring me some tea.

How much care and kindness he had shown me, more than he had shown all the winter bathers—those big, tan, athletic strangers. I was covered with freckles, frightfully skinny, fair, and never to be tan. In a white hat and sunglasses, my foot never touching the water, my hand never holding that frightful beach paddle, I was protected by the chairkeeper. He fiercely sheltered me like an eagle hovering over its young: that fair fledgling that had drifted from the city and wintered among the fishes and dolphins on "his," Moishe the chairkeeper's, piece of shore.

But the man standing over me in the shop was not Moishe. And he had no intention of sheltering me. He cast his bloodshot eyes at me, totally indifferent. An old drunkard. What have I to do with your stale heap of antiques? I will rummage around a bit and leave. Over there, in the corner, on a silly-looking green velvet couch, lies a long gray wooden box with two metal handles. I will ask its price and then, so as not to anger the storekeeper, will buy it and be off. As if I had come all this way only to buy that box. I will take it home and present it to Edward as a gift. He can use it for his seven recorders. After all, he has seven recorders, but no case, chest, nor even a box in which to keep them.

"How much?" I asked casually. I can never walk out of a store empty-handed. I have always been terrified of storekeepers. Ever since then.

"Twenty dollars," he bellowed.

Ha, who do you think you are that I should bargain with you? Even if I am nothing more to you than a bony bag of limbs and freckles, a stray Jewess, I am the daughter of kings, and my ancestors reigned in Jerusalem in the days of Uzziah, Yotham, Ahaz, and Hezekiah!

"Twenty dollars, it's a deal!" I answered with ease, loud and clear. But as I took hold of the sides of the box to carry it with me, it felt heavy.

I lifted the lid. The box was filled with thick, old glass slides. Well, these were quite easy to dispose of. As soon as I was out of the shop, I would dump them in the large garbage can by the door. But a curious sense of pride urged me to show "him" that I had no fear, that I was a free woman, independent, and so I would leave his store stepping proudly, taking my time. I pulled out one of the slides and lazily raised it to the bare bulb that dangled from the ceiling. Against the light, and through the slide, looking down at me very clearly, was the double gate, the sealed one. Yes, that very gate! Those arched twins of a gazelle. Yes, yes! The Golden Gate—the Gate of Mercy.

With a longing hand I drew out another slide. Just one more. The New Gate! From the inside. In the sentry box stands a guard in breeches and leggings, with a turban. A Turk. A Turkish sentry! The box in my hands was old. An antique. The slides were of thick glass. First of their kind. Hurry up and get out of here, quick, before he realizes the loot you've just come upon. That old scoundrel, in a minute he will begin to wonder what sort of treasure I just bought from him for thirty shekels.

*Yes, that very gate! Those arched twins of a gazelle. Yes, yes! The Golden Gate—the Gate of Mercy.*

The box was tucked under my arm, and a vague smile was on my face. Ha, the cunning one! I made my way to the door as slowly as possible, while the tune that had haunted me since this morning was humming wildly in my head: "I am athirst, I am athirst. . . ." There, almost at the door. I gave a lampshade a casual brush, patted the top of a plump glass bowl, and was on my way out. Homeward. To the slides. But the entrance was blocked by the tall frame of Bob Alistair, the auctioneer from Alistair and Son, Used Furniture & Antiques. This Bob was a graceless man, with a square, hollow-cheeked face and a rusty voice. He was always dressed in black, like a mortician. But once I saw him in the auction hall.

In that hall, once the audience is seated, the auctioneer is the king. People entering the room are immediately taken over by a spirit of madness and feel compelled to put their good money on all the bargains, as if it were their last chance. They all try very hard to find favor in the eyes of the auctioneer, and I suspect that this is the sole reason for their indiscriminate buying. He calls out a price, and their hands go up in the air; he raises it, and up go their hands again; and he keeps on, without end.

Once, while sitting there, I lost control over my hand and could trust it no more. It had just lifted itself up to

*The New Gate! From the inside. In the sentry box stands a guard in breeches and leggings, with a turban. A Turkish sentry!*

correct my glasses, but no one could have vouched that this motion was not a bid. And since my right hand had lost its credibility, I was forced to lower my head to my knees just to fit my glasses on my nose.

The end of that day is lost to memory.

Now Bob Alistair was standing over me, his body blocking the entrance, and he was smiling at me with his hollow cheeks, ridiculing me. What did he want? After all, this was not his store. What had he to do with this place? The slides were mine! What else? His? His inheritance? Had he inherited them? And who had deeded them? Aha! In a minute he would claim that since they had come here from his auction hall, he had a right to them. That indeed they were his. That he had inherited them from his grandfather.

And who was his grandfather?

Wait a minute. Oy! Hiram Alistair.

A Bostonian. A pilgrim to the Holy Land. At the end of the nineteenth century.

The rustle of dry leaves at the shop's entrance whispered in my ears; the warm autumn breeze stroked my face. But Bob was still standing over me, at the shop's entrance. Smiling. Ridiculing me. His grandfather's smile, Hiram Alistair's, hovered mockingly over his lips.

*H*iram Alistair was forty when he picked up a newspaper in the reading room of Boston's St. Aiden's Church, and read about the Prince of Wales's journey to the Holy Land, accompanied by his royal photographer, the renowned Francis Bedford. Hiram Alistair read the article and was forever robbed of his peace of mind. For weeks he sent letters and notes to all whom the matter might concern, as well as to his business associates in Boston. He settled his affairs, kissed his wife and son, and boarded a ship that sailed to London.

He arrived in Jerusalem in the spring of 1888, eager to absorb the sights of the Holy Land and to photograph them. He planned, in time, to show them in crowded Boston church auditoriums, accompanied by a narration of his fabulous adventures. Like one of the illustrious voyagers of old.

Alas, Hiram Alistair spoke no other language but his native English, and of the customs of the land and its inhabitants he knew nothing at all. And so it was not wise to have walked out of his hotel, anxiously and enthusiastically, at high noon on his first day in the city, equipped with a small Bible bound in blue cloth, a heavy tripod, and an enormous camera in a leather case strung over his shoulder. No sooner had he stepped out, than a strong east wind greeted him, carrying clusters of filthy, rheumy-eyed and fly-infested boys. Sneezing, their noses oozing, they swarmed around him with outstretched hands.

Hiram Alistair stood there in his white trousers gathered into shiny gaiters, a tropical hat on his head. He stood there, preaching before them, in the heat of the day. How was it that they were not in school at this time of the day? Huh? And why hadn't they washed their hands? And did their parents know that they were begging in the streets?

Before too many days had passed, the waifs and strays, all of them, came to realize that the American was harmless; that he was not of lordly manner; and that he was a miser. Little by little, they washed their hands of him. Left without a guide, Hiram Alistair dragged himself around, day after day, the sun beating upon him mercilessly. Dazed, he wandered the streets, snapping pictures, as if moonstruck. Rivers of perspiration washed him by day, and his bowels tormented him by night.

One morning, in his hotel, he learned about the old inscription two schoolboys had come upon deep inside a tunnel in the Valley of Kidron. He immediately resolved to see it with his own eyes, to touch it with his very hands, and to walk through the tunnel with his very legs. *Were not the rest of the deeds of Hezekiah, and all his might, and how he made the pool, and the conduit, and brought water into the city, were they not written in the Book of Chronicles of the kings of Judah?*

Hiram Alistair stood at the steps leading to Gihon Spring in his immaculate white trousers, his gaiters, and his tropical hat, the little blue Bible in his hand. Three boys who had been standing there joined him, trying to persuade him to buy lighted candles from them before descending into the depths of the tunnel. As he rebuked them in English for their truancy and the cost of the candles, he neglected to notice their hand signals, which were warning him that on such a warm day the water in the tunnel rises up to a man's shoulders. Hiram Alistair did not heed their warnings, and with an upright bearing, he descended the steps to the mouth of the tunnel. In his left hand he carried the candle for light, and in his right, the Book of Books. When he reached the bottom of the steps, where the boys could see him no more, he leaned against the wall, took off his boots, tied them together, hung them by their laces around his neck, and disappeared into the tunnel. He immediately sank to the waist in cold, murky water.

Slowly he moved away from the opening, his bare feet plodding in the gurgling, polluted tunnel bed. Thus he walked, the darkness overpowering him, the water mounting all around him. Then the ceiling came down upon him, as it was rather low in that part of the tunnel, and he bent and lowered his head. The foul waters rose and came to his chest, and the gaiters that hung from his shoulders smacked against the water.

As he dragged on, slimy particles began to pass between his bare toes. Some sort of algae? Or could it be

seaweed? Or leeches? Leeches were devouring his toes, clasping round and round his ankles. The scream that rose in his throat came out sounding like a bleating twitter. He tried to turn back, but he had gone too far, and darkness closed in on him from that side as well. Then the water abated, and he straightened himself up a bit and stopped for a moment to rest the sole of his foot. He was seized by itching from his toes to his knees; the muscles in his thighs twitched wildly. A thin wail rising and subsiding in his throat, he continued walking, straining to widen his steps, struggling to come out, out of the bowels of the tunnel. He raised his eyes, hoping to glimpse a ray of light at the opening, and was struck on the head. The ceiling of the tunnel was very low there. His tropical hat fell off and was lost in the current of vile water that rushed past him, up to his neck.

And then a horrible howl, like the cry of the wilderness of the sea, sounded from one end of the tunnel to the other. It intensified until it became a dreadful roar: *Ye have made also a ditch between the two walls for the water of the old pool. But ye have not looked unto the maker thereof, neither respect him who fashioned it long ago?* And the candle flickered. With a continuous wail, Hiram Alistair put the Bible in his mouth and sheltered the candle with his right hand. And he moved on very slowly,

*In the pool outside the tunnel a group of Arab boys wearing only their underwear was splashing in the water.*

so that the flame would not go out and the Bible not depart from between his clenched teeth.

Afterwards the water receded, the ceiling moved further away, and a pale light darted in, along with the sounds of boys' laughter. A lone dog was barking in the distance, one of the dogs of the village of Siloam. In the pool outside the tunnel a group of Arab boys wearing only their underwear was splashing in the water. They were caressing and teasing each other playfully, shouting with joy. Suddenly they caught sight of Hiram Alistair coming out of the tunnel. He was wailing and gasping as he climbed the step that led to the pool. His body was shaking, his eyes were bulging out of their sockets, and he seemed to be sinking under the yoke of his water-filled boots. The rollicking voices died down for a moment, but the water-hole dwellers soon revived and took to jeering the man. Pretending to come to his aid, they signaled him to move to the right end of the pool, where the water was deepest, and into which the sewage traveled. The hapless one sank to his chin. And he who climbed out of the pit cursed them in the name of the Lord, all forty-two boys.

A cool evening breeze began to blow, and shadows descended on the pool. A dull pain was gnawing at his loins; a reddish rash was spreading over his cheeks. Hiram Alistair sat on the step and vomited the water from the pool into the pool.

The boys' laughter diminished slowly, blending with the bleating of goats and the lone barking that came from the direction of the village. And the excess water from the pool flowed into the King's Garden, where gigantic fig trees swayed and clapped softly, softly. . . .

When Hiram Alistair woke to the cry of the water peddler who was coming up from Ein Ayyub with the waterskins over his shoulders, his eyes burned, his temples throbbed, and dark pink blotches covered his face and neck. He took hold of the railing, staggered up the steps, turned to the right and cried out. The astonished water carrier stared after him until he disappeared into the sloping Kidron Valley, toward Ein Rogel. When he reached the mound by the tree of the prophet Isaiah, Hiram Alistair collapsed. It was there that Yosef Levi found him toward noon on the following day.

Yosef Levi! Who was Yosef Levi?

Well, the noon hour was well under way, and by now I should have returned home, lest Edward worry about me.

And so I smiled back, and Bob Alistair moved to the right most courteously, clearing the entrance for me and wishing me a pleasant day.

Yes, it was a pleasant evening. And warm. Edward lit a fire in the fireplace.

With his wide, wise, quiet hands, he split some twigs and slowly piled them onto a triangular mound, which he encircled with a small rampart made of dried branches. Then he surrounded it with a battery of soft sprigs, on top of which he put three thick logs. Finally, he pushed some dry leaves into the bottom of the pile and kindled the fire.

The fire was crackling softly, the room was filled with warmth, and my heart with remorse. How could I enjoy the evening, how could it please me so, when Hiram Alistair was laid out on the ground, overcome by the heat?

No, he must not be forsaken there, dazed and alone at the foot of the tree, feverish and shivering.

And so it happened that Yosef Levi passed by the tree of the prophet Isaiah, at the crossroad to Ein Rogel. On seeing the American lying faint on the ground, he squatted beside him, and with his wide, warm hands began to wipe the sweat off his forehead and temples. Noticing the pink spots on his cheeks and neck, Yosef Levi went down to the King's Garden and returned with two large figs and a pomegranate. He split each fig in two, placed the cool halves over the man's eyes and temples, and resumed wiping his sweat, this time from his forehead and cheeks.

When the man regained his senses and opened his eyes, Yosef Levi propped him up against the trunk of the tree and sat down beside him. He took the pomegranate in one hand and, with the other, drew a small knife out of a beautifully carved sheath he had made from a hollow branch of a castor-oil plant. He divided the fruit into four segments, discarding the peel, and carefully removed the thin yellow membranes that partitioned the fruit on the inside. He slowly picked out the transparent

*. . . by the tree of the prophet Isaiah, toward Ein Rogel . . .*

red kernels and collected them in his hand. He then shaped his hand like a tube, and the sparkling, ruby-red liquid squirted into the open mouth of the man. Hiram Alistair gargled and shook his head, protesting in English. But Yosef Levi did not know the man's tongue and so remained silent.

He slowly raised his half-closed eyelids. He raised them, fixing Alistair with his gray eyes. A gray so light, it seemed yellow. Yes, splendidly yellow.

Having fed the man kernels of a whole pomegranate, Yosef Levi helped him to his feet and walked him in the direction of the village of Siloam. He guided him into one of the caves in the rocky slopes of the hills overlooking the Valley of Kidron. Inside the cave, he put him on a bed of dried grass sewn into a striped sheet of many colors, and nursed him there for four days and three nights.

Yosef Levi was eight years old when he came with his father and several other families from Yemen to live in the Holy City. They had come there, as was written, because *they held her stones dear, and had pity on her dust*. It was in the year 1882.

The newcomers were pitiful and destitute, their sufferings too hard to bear. They were abandoned, and no one seemed to care. They languished in poverty until an American gentleman, the founder of the American Colony on the hilltop, took pity on them and saved them from the shame of starvation. By then, the notables of Jerusalem also took pity on their wretched brethren, and they helped them settle in the village of Siloam, where they farmed the land and subsisted from it in dignity.

Yosef's mother did not reach the Holy City. She had died on the way, just a short distance from their destination. The father did not know how to care for his son. The boy grew up unattended, the only one among the Jewish children free from the study of Torah and the burden of the Talmud. His father had given up on him in conscious resignation, deeming him *a lad with the sons of Bilhah and Zilpah,* who ran around all day, playing in the streets with the Arab boys.

And the boy grew up, his complexion like honey, his earlocks fairer than those of the rest of the Yemenite children, and his arched eyelids always lowered halfway over his eyes. But when he occasionally raised them, he revealed a pair of yellow eyes, naked of expression, yet lending a certain sense of peace to those around him. They were clear eyes, yellow, seeing and not seen.

The boy wandered about the streets and courtyards of Siloam, day in and day out, always coming back to the door of Hacham Nehunia's house. There he helped out with the daily chores—carrying the water from the cistern, mopping the floors, milking the goat, and running errands for Haya, Hacham Nehunia's wife, for it was she who gave him some bread and olives, or a slice of cheese.

And every now and then, the young woman dipped the bread in an aromatic stew and gave it to him, and the bread in his hand would be seasoned with onion and garlic gravy, warm and golden.

Yosef was not particularly friendly or outgoing toward the little ones, hers or the neighbors', who crawled and quarreled at the doorway and around the courtyard. He never picked any of them up, nor greeted them with laughter, nor told them fairy tales. But they always fixed their eyes on him and followed him around whenever he came and went.

Once, at the beginning of autumn after the first rain, he picked the blossom of a plant called the Rod of Aaron, into which raindrops had collected, and he also picked up a large snail from the ground. He put the snail on the palm of his hand and tipped the calyx toward its opening. One by one, the raindrops fell on the grayish crust that covered the snail's opening, which turned, little by little, right before the children's eyes, into a dark grayish mush. Suddenly the soft mass rose and became a moist corpuscle, growing out of the shell. And it slowly sprouted into the shape of a head. Then a pair of antennae burst forth from its top, growing longer until they reached their full size, and at the end of each, a tiny black globule was sparkling. With his finger, Yosef motioned to the children to remain perfectly still, and he carefully laid the creature on the ground. Within a very short time the children saw a silver train forming before them, the kind produced by the snail's mucus on sunny winter days.

And there was the time when he brought them a small sac that had been extracted from the insides of a fish in the marketplace. He had picked it up from the ground, where it lay discarded. Yosef washed it well and sat down in the yard, and was immediately surrounded by a group of small children with brown, eager eyes.

He drew his knife out of its carved sheath, and with his calm fingers peeled off the outer layers of the fish's sac, trimming away the excess veins, until it appeared dazzlingly transparent. Double-winged, it was the color of mother-of-pearl, taut and proud. Yosef chose a good-looking puddle in the yard and set the sac sailing on its water. For the rest of that day the twin-sailed vessel cruised the water, and the children remained beside the puddle, and there was peace till evening.

Yosef's wanderings took him to faraway places. There were times when his path led him to the Garden of Gethsemane, where, for one reason or another, the keeper's children let him watch them play. It was a miracle that they hadn't taunted that strange, silent boy, with the fair earlocks that dangled from both sides of his head. For many days Yosef came and went. The keeper's children grew accustomed to his standing in the distance, and, in time, he silently joined them in their games, returning to his father's house in the village at dusk.

Once he sat on the ground, leaning against the trunk

of the giant olive tree that grew in the Garden of Geth-semane, preparing to carve a large, beautiful pine cone.

The keeper's children came and sat beside him.

First he pulled out of his pocket a rectangular gray stone whose center was concave from use. He spat on it twice, drew his knife out of its sheath, and began to sharpen it on the stone. Back and forth, back and forth, the squeaking sounds sending chilling waves through the boys' arms and necks, to the edge of their teeth. Then he passed the blade over the soft part of his thumb and, pleased with its sharpness, placed the stone on the ground and began whittling the stem of the pine cone. He shaved and whittled it, shaping it into a beautiful beak. Then he turned the pine cone and began, very carefully, to carve circles around each of its knobs. He peeled white streaks in them until a lovely peacock emerged from between his serene fingers, right before the children's eyes.

Yosef decided to make the peacock a pair of legs, so he picked himself two twigs from the ground and began to peel them.

And suddenly, like a curtain, night had fallen.

A spark of malice flashed through one of the boys, and he picked up a dry branch of an olive tree, narrow and sinuous, and placed it surreptitiously behind Yosef's

*He sat on the ground, leaning against the trunk of the giant olive tree that grew in the Garden of Gethsemane.*

back. He signaled his friend to get up, and he himself started to scream:

"A snake, ya Yousuf, a snake! A SNAKE!"

And he fled, dragging his friend behind him. Yosef turned around, and on seeing the grayish serpentine creature lying behind him, he wanted to run. But his legs, which had been folded under him Indian style, made it difficult. The boys in the meantime were on the run, laughing, and Yosef was screaming and struggling to get up. The cries that tore from his heart brought people out of their homes in the surrounding area. When Yosef finally got up, he started running at a frightfully slow pace toward the monastery at Gethsemane crying out wild cries. The monastery's Arab housekeeper came out of the building and, on seeing the child, she saw at once that he had lost his senses.

Could he be epileptic? She rushed to him. No, that was not an epileptic seizure. He was simply seized by fear.

People had already gathered around him, and the boy was screaming and crying. The old woman looked around until she caught sight of the two lads in the distance, their laughter slowly fading.

She took the child by the hand and walked over to the boys and asked them in her well known and knowing voice what had happened to Yosef. Then, as the child still cried out beside her, she said, "Come, Yousuf, let's go. Let's take a look at the snake." And she took him to the giant olive tree. She pointed to the gray gnarled branch: "Here Yousuf, here's the snake-that-is-not-a-snake. A branch of the ancient olive tree." And she repeated that several times and sat down on the ground at the foot of the tree. Little by little his screams diminished until they ceased, and he looked around as if he had just come back from a distant land. And he hiccuped.

Afterwards she gave him some bread and had her eldest son, Ibrahim, take him back to the village of Siloam, to the Jewish neighborhood. And the child walked, hiccuping and taking bites from his bread, until they reached his father's house. And it was from then on that he began his excursions to the monastery garden, where he helped Um Ibrahim with her chores and returned home before nightfall.

One day, on his way to the garden, Yosef saw from a distance that she was bent over an Arab child, holding his leg. The child's mother was standing beside him, uttering a continuous, spiraling warble with her voice. When Um Ibrahim saw him coming down the path she stopped what she was doing and waited for him to get close to her. While Yosef stood by her side, she took the boy's leg in her hands once again, feeling the swollen heel with her fingers. It had a large green abscess on it. The old lady took a kitchen knife and a glass bead. She held them together and passed them over the sore. And she repeated her action.

She then sprinkled the sore with some water, placed over it a dressing of white petals from the blossom of the sambuccus tree that grew in the yard, and turned to the fire that was burning in the clay hearth outside the kitchen. There she grilled a whole large onion. When the onion was well done, she boiled it in water seasoned with cottonseeds. She then mashed the onion into a paste which she applied to the sore, dressing it finally with a grape leaf. She bandaged it tightly, fastening it with a piece of old cloth. And all the while, whenever there was a lull in the mother's ululation, Um Ibrahim filled it with her smooth deep voice. And she called the various plants by their names, enumerating their healing qualities and pointing to their benefits.

On the following day, when the abscess would open, she would concoct a cure from the leaves of the romero plant, which is none other than the squill plant and is known to contain fifty-two remedies. She would grind the leaves into a fine powder, which she would then sprinkle over the wound, and the opening would close. And with the help of the cobwebs that she would spread over the heel, the sore would heal, and the boy would recover.

Yosef nodded his head silently, his yellow eyes opened wide. When Um Ibrahim straightened herself up at last she saw him standing there, moved, his eyes fully exposed. She smiled at him fondly, a cunning smile. The smile of an accomplice.

And Yosef returned to the village with light steps. It was the Thursday before Shabbat Hagadol, the Great Sabbath that precedes Passover, and Haya, Hacham Nehunia's wife, stood in the courtyard piling the laundry into large heaps under the olive tree. The large copper kettle and washtub were warming in the sun. It seemed that the young woman had designated that day to do her wash for the coming holiday. There was a hole in the ground next to the kettle, and there were three large charred stones around its opening. Yosef walked over there and positioned them properly. He then raked the hole with his fingers, turned to gather anything he could find for the fire, and stooped over the hole.

With his wide, wise, quiet hands he split some twigs and slowly piled them into a triangular mound, which he encircled with a small rampart made of dried branches. Then he surrounded it with a battery of soft sprigs, on top of which he put three thick logs. Finally, he pushed some dry leaves into the bottom of the pile and kindled the fire. Next he took hold of the fine-bellied copper kettle by its handles and placed it on the stones. He drew water from the cistern and poured it into the kettle and the washtub. Then, contrary to his custom, he turned and entered the house.

Haya put the wash in the kettle to boil. She sprinkled yellow soap flakes over the water and stood there, stirring with a smooth pole of olive wood. The hours passed, and she kept on mixing and boiling, hoisting steaming sails of laundry with her stick and dropping them into the tub. When Hacham Nehunia's wife finally went into the house, she was astonished at the sight of the boy standing against the windowsill, absorbed in one of her husband's books. Could he have learned to read while in Yemen? she wondered. And she tiptoed out of the room. The hour grew late, the shadows longer, and it was time for Hacham Nehunia to return from his daily occupations. Haya went back into the room and gave Yosef a slice of bread dipped in olive oil. Then Yosef left for his father's house.

Outside the wash had already been hung over the olive tree branches, and the courtyard was enveloped in the smell of smoke, while in the hole a smoldering fire crackled into embers. . . . Just as when the neighborhood women, Mother among them, would cleanse the dishes for Passover. They would chide us for playing idly in the sand, urging us to go and wash up. Evening was approaching, they would say, and what sort of a Seder would we have, fooling around as we did?

That marvelous smoke. That sweet fragrance everywhere, the fragrance of Passover, reaching every corner, and smoldering fire crackling into embers . . .

Yes, what sort of a Seder is it, ha? And why have all these people suddenly assembled here? It seems they are about to have a communal Seder. But they are not reading the right passages from the Haggadah. What has come over them? Ignoramuses, who do not know how to conduct a Seder properly. I am getting out of here. Father, Father, wait for me. I am coming home. What's happening? What is the matter with you, Father? How come we are not having a Seder this year, and these people, these ignoramuses have joined together to make themselves a mock Seder?

All the way home a protest is rising in me, which I will hurl at Father as soon as I walk in the door. On my way I peek into windows and see that the candles are lit and Seders are being conducted by people seated around festive tables. I look in and see Mr. London, and Kornfeld, and Kirshman, and old Mr. Sirkin. But they are all among the dead now. They died long ago; I know that. And as I walk into our house I no longer speak to Father or Mother. Overcome by anger, I retreat at once to the "small room" and collapse onto the bed. To sleep.

Then my Aunt Haya tiptoes in—she, too, is long dead—and she moves toward my bed with a slipper in her hand, and she is laughing as she is about to slap at the heels of my feet with it. My heels stick up because I am sleeping on my stomach and my legs are folded, in an inverted Indian style. She is moving closer, laughing, about to strike me, and, horrified, I begin to scream, awful screams.

The terrible cry that tore out of my throat woke up Edward, who was sleeping on the sofa beside me, across from the fire. Edward stroked my head, brushed my hair with his wise, wide-fingered, innocent hand. He asked me: "Again? What did you dream of now? God only knows. Won't you tell me about it?" And I did.

And he asked me for more. He asked me to dive into the bottom and root of that horror, that fear. When? And from where?

Oh yes. Yes, when I was seven. "The Snake Tale." Every member of my family is familiar with this tale. To this day I can't bear the sight of a snake. Not even in a picture. Or in a glass cage in the zoo. Or, for that mat-

ter, any crawling creature that creeps on the earth. These
things are ancient.

Edward asked me to tell him about the snake episode.

The Snake Tale:

Once, Zieva, Yael, and I were sitting on the sand behind our house, playing. We were about six or seven
years old. My legs were folded under me Indian style,
which made it difficult to get up. And we played in
the sand.

Suddenly, like a curtain, night had fallen.

A spark of malice flashed through Zieva. She took a
piece of frayed elastic band and placed it on the ground
behind my back. Next, she got up, and dragging Yael
behind her she started to scream, as though petrified.

"A snake! A snake! A SNAKE! . . ."

This is the Snake Tale, Edward. *And I have heard it
said of you that when you hear a dream you can interpret it.*
And he listened to me quietly, and then he asked me
softly:

"You, with all your ancient Semitic languages, how do
you say snake in Arabic?"

And I answered him promptly, "Haya."

The word had barely left my lips when my entire
body began to tremble. A new scream mounted in my
throat, but I managed to hold it back.

Haya, my poor aunt Haya, who had never harmed
me or anyone else, had had the honor of entering my
dream by virtue of her name alone. Haya—the snake—

moved in on me, ready to strike my heel, as it is written: *He shall bruise your head, and you shall bruise his heel.* These things are ancient.

Edward stroked my head, stroked it, a sad peace flowing from his hand into my hair, head, neck, into my blood. His stroking hand was growing heavy. Edward had fallen asleep. Sh. . . .

*S*h . . . Pst . . . Hey, Yosef Levi! Are you sleeping? Or are you scared to? Are you scared the nightmare will return to haunt you? Yes, my son, I know. For *from the serpent's root will come forth an adder, and its fruit will be a flying serpent.* Do listen to me, my son. In one of Hacham Nehunia's books there is a marvelous amulet. And so, from this day on, you must stop wandering about the alleys of the village and its courtyards, the slopes of Kidron and its caves. You must instead go to Hacham Nehunia's house every day and lean against the sill of the window overlooking the valley. And there you must read and read, all of his books, scrolls, and documents. You must read through the morning, noon, and afternoon, until the wise man's wife enters and gives you some bread and olives. Or a piece of cheese. And sometimes she will even dip it in a stew, and the bread in your hand will be seasoned with onion and garlic gravy, warm and golden. And in one of the books you will come upon a letter written as follows:

"There once was a man from Safed who had been sent to the Land of Yemen to collect alms for the poor of the Holy Land. And he stopped in the city of San'a for several days. And on each of these days he espied a certain man, tall and eminent, who seemed to command the respect of all who saw him. And the emissary from the Holy Land asked the people of the city who that certain man might be, whence had he come, and which was his native land. For the man's garments and manner were unlike those of the local people. And their word was that the man had come to their city only a few days before, saying that he hailed from the Tribe of Dan. And the Danite was handsome and good-looking, strong and lofty; his eyes were blazing, his luxurious beard long and flowing, his locks, black as a raven, cascading down his back. His raiment seemed like that worn by the people from the East. He tied a long, wide belt around it, into which holy sayings in the Hebrew tongue were woven. One said: *Dan shall be a serpent in the way, a viper by the path.* Girded to his thigh was a large, wide sword, and his tongue was pure Hebrew. But he spoke very little, thinking a while before uttering a single sound. He ate very little, bread and water only, and slept two or three hours at a time, and he washed himself in water many times during the course of a day. His customs and ways were much like those of the Nazirites, also known as the

Essenes, renowned in the book of the messianic priest Josephus Flavius and the scholar Philo the Alexandrine.

"And when the envoy from Safed asked the Danite about the members of his tribe, he replied very briefly, saying that they were living in peace and tranquility always. Their kingdom was vast, several months' walk from the city of San'a. And the Yemenites were greatly amazed, for they could not understand how it was possible for the Danite to have crossed the awesome desert alone, where the snakes and the scorpions dwelt. Surely it was the blessing of our holy father Jacob, which he had bestowed upon the tribe of Dan just before his death. This blessing alone protects all of his descendants, warding snakes and serpents off their path."

Now Yosef, my son, this is what you must do. Make yourself a belt like that of the eminent and holy Danite, and his virtue will protect you, and you shall be safe from the wrath of all things creeping on the ground by day and from terrifying dreams by night.

In the last watch of that night my sleep was very pleasant. And the days born of that night were also lovely. They came and went lazily, the holidays passed, and I lived in peace.

And then, by the end of that autumn, the ones in charge at Brandeis University appointed me to teach there, and the slides were left to rest like stones unturned for many months and years.

$A$nd what of Yosef, through all those months and years?

Yosef stayed off the paths of the village and its alleys, the slopes of Kidron and its hidden caves. But he did go every day to Hacham Nehunia's house, where he stood near the window overlooking the valley and read the books. He read and read, until it was almost time for Hacham Nehunia to return from his daily occupations. It was then that the wise man's young wife would hasten to give Yosef a slice of bread, which he took and departed.

The only other place he continued to visit was the courtyard of the monastery. There he lent a hand to Um Ibrahim. And more often than not, he happened along when the sick and afflicted were being brought in.

And they came. One with a head injury, another with a dislocated arm, one with a prolapsed eye, another with a fractured leg. They all came up the paths leading to Um Ibrahim's monastery.

And she was like a book of remedies that had been long concealed but were now revealed. She blended and concocted, crushed and ground, smoked and milled, bandaged and anointed. And if Yosef happened by during her ministrations, Um Ibrahim worked in a way that afforded him a full view of her actions, which she accompanied with her smooth, deep voice. She named every plant and herb, enumerated their healing qualities, expounded on the various combinations of medicines and dressings and on the virtues of the elixirs. Moved, Yosef stood there, nodding his head, absorbing everything, missing nothing.

Only much later, stammering, did he begin to unfold before her all that he had read in the books, and she listened with a cunning smile, the smile of an accomplice.

And her compassionate brown eyes never failed to notice that the lad was always in a hurry to leave before dark. Before dark, and with broad strides. With his eyes fixed on the ground, and his ears open to every rustle among the thorns.

On the day he was fifteen, he went to the abandoned shack in Bir Ayyub in the direction of Ein Rogel. It was there, right at the entrance to the shack, that he found a wide strip of leather. He sat down on the ground and inscribed on it with his knife the words, *Dan shall be a serpent in the way, a viper by the path*. He girded the belt around his waist and walked, encouraged, up the path leading to the village. Only he did not remember, or notice, that the holy man of whom he had read in the letter was of the tribe of Dan, while he, Yosef Levi, was a Levite.

He walked on, quickly. Suddenly he turned around and headed for the garden of Gethsemane.

As he was coming up the path from one direction, a pitiful looking girl was coming from the other. She was holding a wailing toddler by the hand whose free arm

dangled at his side like a rag. She slowly climbed the
steps leading from the valley.

And out of the window peered Um Ibrahim, and she
smiled.

Was she hinting at Yosef to approach the child?

Whatever the case, Yosef heeded her smile and walked
down the path innocently, as if he were going down just
for the sake of going down. He walked, observing the
toddler who whined and cried, studying the arm that
was hanging loosely from the shoulder. They met on one
of the narrow steps, and Yosef blocked the passage. As
the girl tried to pass him on his right, Yosef took hold of
the astonished child, seizing him by his skinny shoulder
with one hand and by his dangling arm, just above the el-
bow, with the other. And then, in one quick, vigorous motion, he simultaneously pulled, stretched, and rotated.
The dislocated arm went back into place with a dull
clicking sound. And in the vacant yard of the monastery,
the child's final wail resounded, bewildered, unfinished.

Then Yosef pulled out of his pocket two polished
marbles and rolled them on the ground. The child cut
himself loose from his sister's grip, dropped on all fours,
and tried to catch them with his two hands. The small
transparent glass globes rolled in the sun, trailing behind them tails of antique red light, and Yosef slowly
raised his eyelids, shyly. Um Ibrahim was still standing

*Toward Ein Rogel.*

by her window. The smile in her eyes deepened, to the point of pain. Then a hint of a smile marked the edge of Yosef's lips as well.

Yosef, who was most reticent, suddenly moved in front of Um Ibrahim's window and started telling her about Hezekiah, king of Judah. Whatever possessed him to do so? He stood there, telling her all about the book of remedies King Hezekiah had concealed, and how much the sages thanked him for having done so. And as he talked, his hands caressed the pots and vessels.

For standing on the windowsill were many pots and vessels, jars and cruses and jugs *bringing forth vegetation, plants yielding seed each according to its kind.* Just as on the third day of the Creation, when the earth brought forth thousands upon thousands of different kinds of plants and grasses, and not one of them without its merits and strength.

And she, the old one, the wise one, stood there, leaning on the windowsill with her elbows, *as if she were set up, at the first, before the beginning of the earth.* She had built her home, poured her wine, set her table, and grew every kind of weed and plant in pots and vessels all around her. Like the righteous Noah in his time. Noah, who had been called upon by the angel Raphael to minister to the sick and care for them with every kind of

*And around the courtyard were rows upon rows of containers bringing forth vegetation, plants yielding seed each according to its kind.*

tree that grew in the earth, and every kind of plant that came forth from the soil. And he had learned all about their healing properties, their merits and virtues in restoring the ill back to health and to life.

And Noah had written all of those things in a book and gave it to his son, Shem. And that was the book Hezekiah the king had used.

And now, on the windowsill and on top of the stone fences and around the courtyard were rows upon rows of containers *bringing forth vegetation, plants yielding seed each according to its kind.*

And in her kitchen too. Yes. Rows upon rows of:
Jars, tubes, and flagons of glass
filled with salts, balms, and many a spice,
sweet herbs, perfumes, elixirs,
and aromatic resins from the balsam firs.
Almonds, honeyed tragacanth and ladanum,
millet, stacte, onycha and galbanum,
Cloves, frankincense, nard and saffron,
calamus, sage, marjoram and cinnamon.
Yes. And myrrh and aloes, basil and thyme,
And even a *hin* of oil and a measure of wine.

And to her spikes of oats, ears of corn, mushrooms, and sprouts, Yosef would add the powders he had read about. He would buy them in Sook el-Atareen, the Perfumers' Market inside the city walls.

And he went on helping her, often staying around to assist her. And she let him. First grinding and beating the herbs into fine powders. Then compounding and mixing them. And little by little she entrusted her wretched patients into his hands. If he happened to be in the yard while she was in the kitchen, they all came to him. First with a tooth and an eye. Or even an ear.

Like that small child, whose mother had already hung a horse's tooth around his neck, yet whose pain had not subsided. He came crying to Yosef. And Yosef took some leaves of the squill plant, burned them, and placed the ashes in a white cloth with which he rubbed the child's sore gums. And it helped.

Afterwards he took the tendril of the redbud blossom, dipped it in some rose honey, and applied it gently to the child's gums. And it helped. Yes, it helped. And Yosef was happy. It seemed that nothing stood between his patient and himself. Neither a wail nor a whimper, not a sigh nor a savage roar. Only Yosef and the patient's affliction. He and the sore. He and the inflamed gum. He and the oozing eye . . .

Water secreted by the dill weed is a good eye remedy. And so he washed the infected eye in dill water, and afterwards he simmered lentils in wine, blended in some oils and chicory juice, and prepared an eye dressing. And it helped.

Once he came running.

Um Ibrahim had never seen him run before.

When he got there he stopped, panting. He had just read that the young of the falcon, the young of the falcon—if you climbed up to their nest and took one—took a fledgling and blinded it with a needle and then returned it to its place, and waited around for about half a day or a bit more, and climbed up to the nest once again—you would see that the young bird had been blinded. And the grass its mother would have used to restore its sight would be lying in the nest. And if she, Um Ibrahim, would take that grass, take it and use it, the eyes would heal!

Um Ibrahim watched the agitated boy for a long while and kept her silence. Afterwards she casually remarked that the gall of a bull, when thoroughly mixed with honey and spread over the eyes, would also heal.

And the bewildered Yosef stood there, embarrassed, then turned around and returned to the village. He didn't go back to the monastery for many days. But when he did, the warm, playful smile was rekindled in her eyes. And she taught him a marvelous way to cure headaches.

And her smile seemed to tease: How about it, ya Yousuf? I've still got a cure or two in my bag, haven't I, ya Yousuf, my precious?

Apple of my eye.

W hy were the eyes of the children of Hacham Nehunia's wife always so infected? Weak and bleary and watery? She, whose eyes were like black silk curtains, their black—the world, their white—the ocean that encircles it. Like the pools in Heshbon bathed in milk.

But her children?

Yosef would stand over them silently, washing their eyes, dressing them, bandaging them. Their father had already told his neighbors in the synagogue: "Yosef's heart is a locked garden. *A garden locked, a fountain sealed.* But his hands—his hands are the hands of Asaf."

And the word spread, and people in the village were saying, "His hands are the hands of Asaf."

And the hands were the hands of Asaf the Healer.

And the toddlers who crawled on the ground, at the doorstep, and in the courtyard minded Yosef and heeded his silence.

They obeyed him when he asked them to open their mouths wide, so that he could see their small tongues and squeeze some lemon drops on them to relieve their sore throats. They obeyed him, those tiny ones who writhed in pain in the evenings, as the worms in their intestines began to torment them. They stood silently every evening, those pitiful little ones, and drank his bitter elixirs.

One spring day the line of suffering children was very long, and their ills were many. Yosef spent most of the noon hours with them in the yard. Finally he asked:

"Is this the last of the lads?"

"There is still the youngest," she said. "He has a toothache."

She spoke to Yosef as she always did.

And his soul failed him when she spoke.

But he stood there, rubbing salve on the baby's gums with warm oil—those sore, decaying gums. Oh, you miserable ones! Vinegar out of wine! Look at your mother's teeth. *All of them bear twins, not one among them is bereaved.* Like a flock of shorn ewes. *Like a flock of ewes that have come up*—and he suddenly stopped. Frozen.

*Flee, my beloved.* Make haste, Yosef. Turn, be like a gazelle, or a young stag upon the Mount of Olives. And run down the slopes of the village of Siloam, to the abandoned shack. Run. To the spot where Nahal Kidron meets the Valley of Hinom leading to Ein Rogel, by the lepers' hospital.

And, indeed, Yosef headed that way.

He hastened his steps. And suddenly, as if from within the strange afternoon light, a bewildering sight unfolded before his eyes.

It was several months since they had begun erecting a church over there, near the Garden of Gethsemane. It was said that the Muscovites were building their house of worship there.

They had been working on it for many months; they had reached the roof line. The domes, however, were still missing—*We have a little sister and she has no breasts.*

*They had begun erecting a church over there, near the Garden of Gethsemane. It was said that the Muscovites were building their house of worship there. They had been working on it for many months; they had reached the roof line. The domes, however, were still missing.*

And Yosef wondered: *What should be done for her on the day when she is spoken for? If she were a wall, they surely would build upon her a battlement of silver.*

Suddenly she ripened. Overnight. Ripened, she towered in all her arched loveliness. Those strange, protruding curves. And admiring herself she said: *I am like a wall and my breasts are like towers.*

Yosef started to run.

He ran and ran, his feet hardly touching the ground. It was as though he were growing taller, rising, soaring.

Suddenly he stopped in his tracks. There was a rustling among the thorn bushes. A scream froze in his throat like a lump of clay: On the ground glistened a slithery black snake.

Only this shrewdest of all creatures, the most accursed, did not crawl upon his belly, but raised himself to half his size.

Legend has it that a Sanhedrin of seventy-one executed the decree against the ancient serpent. He was silenced when his hands and feet were chopped off, and he suffered greatly. His agonized cries went from one end of the world to the other, but his voice could not be heard. And if indeed that one was the first snake, he would get up in no time, and Sammael, Prince of Demons, would come and mount him, for he had chosen him of all creatures to be his friend and accomplice. It must have been that snake, for his bearing was upright!

> *Ripened, she towered in all her arched loveliness. Those strange, protruding curves.*

No, Yosef, no. They are only a pair of snakes. Look, they are joined together in their mating dance.

Yosef stood there, transfixed, his hands gripping, clutching the leather belt around his waist, he couldn't move. His flesh tightened, and his eyes fastened on the snake as if it were a lodestone.

In the meantime, the couple had disengaged themselves and slipped away, he to the right, she to the left, for the whole earth was theirs to roam.

They turned and slithered off.

A heavy weariness settled into Yosef's knees, and he crouched down, panting.

A strange plant was growing there.

Its broad, fleshy leaves were shiny and lay flat on the ground. And in between them there were three stems carrying three bluish-purple blossoms. He had not seen the likes of them before.

He bent over the plant and touched it with his fingertips. The bluish petals felt soft and warm and fuzzy. What could they be?

What could they be?!

Then he saw a fruit ripening among them. A berry-like fruit, juicy and red. Strange of form. He had not seen the likes of it before.

What could it be?!

What?

*Rav said: Mandrake. Rabbi Levi said: A violet. Rabbi Yonatan said: A peony. And the violets are essentially short plants with fragrant flowers.*

The mandrake root is said to be dangerous. It has a cord that extends from its center into the ground and is shaped like a human, and if you take a string and tie one end of the string around an animal's neck and the other end to the mandrake root, and if the animal wrenches it out of the ground, it dies instantly.

What did Reuben do? Reuben tied his donkey to the mandrake root and walked to the fields. On returning, he found the mandrake torn out of the ground and the donkey lying dead. *And Reuben brought the mandrakes to his mother, Leah. Then Rachel said to Leah, "Give me, I pray, some of your son's mandrakes." But she said to her, "Is it a small matter that you have taken away my husband? Would you take away my son's mandrakes too!"*

Oh, do *give me, I pray, give me some of your son's mandrakes . . . that he may lie with you tonight for your son's mandrakes.* Yosef stretched his hand toward the flower, and his heart thrilled within him. He began to stroke the strange flower slowly; it was as soft as down. He brushed his hand over the round fruit, caressed it.

No, *you must come in to me; for I have hired you with my son's mandrakes,* I have hired you, hired-you, you-ooh you-ooh—His hand passed between the curve of the leaves, stroking, and suddenly it plucked the flower and squeezed the fruit. A pungent odor rose from the milky substance that squirted stickily between his fingers.

Yosef lay on the ground and buried his head in the leaves. He lay there crying.

Cry, Yosef; weep, innocent lad. Cry on the mountains: *Cry over the purity of your soul, over all of the tender flowers of your youth.*

> (Alexandria, Scene V)
> *Enter Cleopatra*
> Cleo: Charmian!
> Char: Madam?
> Cleo: Ha, ha!
>      Give me to drink mandragora.
> Char: Why, madam?
> Cleo: That I might sleep out this great gap of time . . .
> *Exit Cleopatra*
> *Exit Cleopatra, but enter Iago.*
> Iago: Look where he comes! Not poppy, nor
>      mandragora,
>      Nor all the drowsy syrups of the world
>      Shall ever medicine thee to that sweet sleep
>      Which thou ow'ds yesterday.

Rise then, Yosef, rise and go down to the Valley of Kidron, to your beloved Ein Rogel. To the tree of the prophet Isaiah. Remember the tale? When Isaiah the prophet fled from King Menasseh, who wanted to kill him, he ran until he reached the carob tree. And the carob opened itself wide and swallowed the prophet. And Menasseh, King of Judah, had woodworkers saw the carob tree, and the blood was dripping. . . . But Isaiah did not cry out, neither did he weep as he was being sawed.

And a mulberry tree is standing there today.

And right beside it, a pile of stones. And when Yosef reached the mound, he found Hiram Alistair lying unconscious there. He revived him and helped him to his feet, and he walked him in the direction of the village of Siloam. He guided him into one of the caves in the rocky slopes of the hills overlooking the Valley of Kidron. Inside the cave he put him on a bed of dried grass sewn into a striped sheet of many colors, and he nursed him there for three nights and four days.

And on the fourth day, Hiram Alistair got up and left. For a while he could be seen wandering about the Khan courtyard of the railway station, and then he disappeared. He was never seen again or heard from in Jerusalem.

And in the cave, among the few articles he had had brought over to him from the hotel and then left behind, there remained a long gray wooden box, with two metal handles. It lay there for many days.

And during those days, Um Ibrahim fell ill.

From a distance still, before he even entered the gate, Yosef could hear the women's voices dissolving into wails— measured, rhythmical wails, for they were trained in lamentation. And at the threshold they crowded around him, each pushing herself in front of the other, to be the first to tell him that, according to the symptoms, Um Ibrahim lay dying. They had already put a pinch of salt in the palm of her hand and waited. And the salt remained dry. Allah have mercy.

Woe—wail.

Yosef walked in gently. He approached the bed, bent over her, and peered into the pupils of her opened eyes. But, indeed, he could not see his reflection in them.

Surely the bitterness of death had passed.

The bitterness of death?

He placed his hand over her forehead very slowly. Her eyes closed, as if confirming the source of pain. Yosef pulled out of his pocket a glass flagon. He pulled it out very carefully, for it contained a most choice cure.

He had worked on it for many days. First he put some leaves from the elder tree inside the container and sealed its mouth with dough. He made sure the leaves did not touch the glass but hung loosely in there. Then he left the container in the sun for two days. Next he removed the old leaves, replaced them with fresh ones, and repeated this action several times until the flagon was filled with a liquid that had been extracted from the elder leaves. This clear liquid was good for severe pain.

Yosef pulled the delicate flask out of his pocket and sprinkled the liquid on her forehead and temples, massaging them with his wise, calm hands.

The hours passed, and he kept on wetting and gently massaging her forehead and temples, as well as her forearms.

It was already past noon when she suddenly opened her eyes and a spark of recognition was kindled in them. She began mumbling, moving her lips, trying to tell him something. Yosef leaned close to her face and seemed to hear her whisper in his ear:

"This one, is this one from Hezekiah the king?"

And he thought he glimpsed a trace of a smile in her eyes. A last flicker of triumphant light.

Strange, as if a tinge of envy had stolen into Yosef's

heart. The cunning one! She's got the upper hand. She was now learning a secret she would never reveal. A secret he would never be able to read about. Not in any of the books.

Wickedly, she was about to take it with her.

The day passed, and on the mountains the hour descended when it was impossible to distinguish between blue and white, one dog from another—they all seemed like wolves. Would Yosef stay over at the monastery?

He would.

Someone lit a candle in the corner of the room. Yosef sat across from it, his legs folded under him. When it burned out, he lit another and contemplated it.

*Who supplies the candles for the light? And those who supply the candles for the light . . . the Holy One, blessed be He, will reward them . . .*

It is said of Rabbi Meir that his name was not Meir—he who shines—but Nehorai—he who enlightens. So why was he called Rabbi Meir? Why? Yosef tried hard to remember but could not, because a song the Ashkenazi children used to sing around the bonfire in Jerusalem possessed his mind:

Cheers, Rabbi Meir, cheers!
Precious oil,
Oil of joy
You have given to your peers. . . .

No, no. That's wrong. That was not the way it went. His name was not Rabbi Meir. What was it?

How strange. There he comes. Rabbi Meir himself, riding his horse on the Sabbath in the marketplace.

Was it Rabbi Meir who had ridden his horse on the Sabbath? The fact is that it was his teacher, Elisha ben Abuyya, who had done so. But the one riding now is none other than Rabbi Meir. And he is coming closer to Yosef, and there is a mocking smile in his kind eyes, mixed with a triumphant light. And he invites Yosef to ride on his shoulders.

And Yosef is already perched up there.

And it is told of Rabbi Shmuel son of Rabbi Nachmani that when he was still a boy he was seated on his grandfather's shoulders going up from his own town to Kefar Hanan via Beth-Shean. And it was there that he heard Rabbi Shimon ben Elazar lecture on the commentary according to Rabbi Meir: *And God saw everything He had made, and behold, it was very good.* In the book of Rabbi Meir it is written: "It is very good (*tov me'od*)—and death is good (*tov mavet*).

Here, death is good.

*T*he voices of the women who had returned at daybreak to continue their chanting awakened Yosef.

A hint of a smile was drawn over his face. Was it possible, he wondered, that Hagar's virtue had stood her,

Um Ibrahim, in good stead, and at the hour of her death that page from the book of Rabbi Meir had been miraculously revealed to her? Was it possible for death to be good? Well, then, death was good.

Yosef left the monastery quickly and turned to go to the shack in the valley by the lepers' hospital, where Nahal Kidron met Bir Ayyub. It was a year since Efrem son of Ingmar had come to live there. Every now and then Yosef went there to help him heap the coals into the furnace and to carry the heavy copper and iron kettles across the yard.

What was Efrem son of Ingmar doing in that place? It was obvious from his name that he belonged to one of the Swedish families who had come to live in the large courtyard of the American Colony uptown. What was he doing at the shack in the valley?

Efrem son of Ingmar was dark and wild.

Efrem, nature's child. Handsome, lean, and agile, like a prince. And dark. What was he doing there in the valley, away from the city? Hadn't he been told that ever since the Ishmaelite water-drawers began hurling stones at anyone who came near the spring, not a single civilized person had dared to live there?

Even the harness-maker from the American Colony, who used to tan his leathers in the spring, stopped going there. Yes, he too had deserted his hut years ago and now it stood there, abandoned. Only some bits of harness and saddle were left scattered about, old leather pieces. What, then, had come over Efrem son of Ingmar that he went to live in that dilapidated shack at Ein Ayyub, at the foot of the Mount of Olives in the direction of Ein Rogel?

True, in the beginning, when he had first come to the Holy Land, he lived with his mother's relatives at the Colony. And his uncle had even taken him to his shop to teach him a trade. He was going to make him his apprentice, a blacksmith's apprentice.

The shop of Olaf son of Ingmar was known all around. The high and mighty used to bring their horses to be shod there.

That is, until Efrem the wild began to apprentice there. For he used to annoy the horses with his laughter, scaring them until they became restless and wild.

What? Had his laughter disturbed only the horses?

His uncle Olaf, as well as the rest of the men in the American Colony who had adolescent daughters, all feared his laughter. That laughter was destined for trouble. A laughter that ruffled the quiet of the nights.

On those nights when he could not sleep, he set out on his nocturnal ramblings. Tortured and haunted by wanderings, he roamed the streets. And the young daugh-

*In the valley by the lepers' hospital, where Nahal Kidron met Bir Ayyub.*

ters trembled in the dark at the echo of his agile steps against the cobblestones. They lay in their beds, longing for that haunting sound, laughter's lamentation, that stirred them so in the night.

Oh, Efrem son of Ingmar. Wild and dark.

Efrem, nature's child. Handsome and lean and agile, like a prince. And dark. His complexion was dark, as was his hair. And his eyes were gray, a very deep gray. And his nimble hands were dark.

And his laughter . . .

Barely a year had passed since his arrival in Jerusalem when he got up and left for that abandoned shack in the valley at Bir Ayyub.

He fixed it up and built a large clay furnace in the yard, which he fitted with a big bellows. He stocked the shack with the best of the land of Zoan. Firewood and glue, a loom and wire spools, and horseshoes and coals. And every now and then Yosef would come and lend him a hand. He would make the fire, blow the large bellows, stir the glue. Not one Swede went to that place near the lepers' hospital, where wild beasts dwelled with hyenas, ostriches with owls, where satyrs danced. Aha! But the villagers' wives—they came.

They assembled by the gate, holding their broken utensils. And he was bent over the fire, naked to his slim waist. Naked and agile, he stood there like a dark rascal, soldering their broken vessels.

Where had all those dark, bony peddlers come from? They somehow impressed themselves into my memory as gypsies. Members of the tribe of Cain. I was around nine when the first one showed up, calling out in a toothless voice: "Mending matta-raasses, koldeh-res, mattaraasses . . ."

He came and parked himself and his wares in the empty lot next to our house. He had with him a harp-like instrument, and he beat large cotton balls in it. He played his harp silently, with those cotton balls.

It was during the Forties, and he traveled from village to village, from one neighborhood to another, making his living mending mattresses and down comforters. Good God! And he had a primus with him, and he cooked something in a small pot on top of it. Something? Glue perhaps? I can only remember the smell, but not what it looked like or for what it was used. What a strange way to make a living. Who had given him mattresses to mend? And what was the difference between mattresses and mattaraasses? And how did one fix "koldehres"—those heavy down comforters covered in faded red satin?

I have forgotten what he looked like. I can only remember his bony cheeks and that I had decided then that he was one of the tent-dwellers, a gypsy.

Gypsy, what a lovely word.

Gypsy, Zoanite. Yes, from the land of Zoan in Eygpt. For the gypsies are indeed descended from the "mixed multitudes" that went up from Egypt with Moses and the people of Israel. And they have a reigning king to this day.

Years later, when I was nineteen and living in Jerusalem, a secondhand clothes peddler knocked on the door and I opened it.

He was lean, tall, tanned, and young. The skin over his handsome high cheekbones was taut, his deep-set black eyes were "blazing." Just as in a novel.

And he stood proudly at the door. A prince! He took the old clothes and gave me a conquering look. For the first time in my life my eyes met a man's. A real man. What more did I need to get up and follow him? For when I was small my mother used to sing:

> When I was sixteen,
> Innocent and green,
> I fell in love
> with a cunning gypsy.
> Woe, what have I done,
> my beautiful dream
> is forever gone
> with a cunning gypsy.

No, I did not follow the gypsy. But Sophie daughter of Ingmar had. Yes, it seemed that she had. How else could that fair, large, and stately Swedish lady have that son, that Efrem, dark and wild, an agile rascal?

Yes.

When she was still a child, she was sent to the country to stay with her relatives. She grew up there, raised in an atmosphere of affluence and gentility. She developed into a quiet, pleasant, and well-bred young woman. Large, fair, and proud.

And then she became pregnant.

And people began to whisper, speculating on who, of all the distinguished gentlemen, could be the father.

But having grown accustomed to respecting her, they did not ask her any questions. And she offered no answers.

She walked with her usual air of dignity, her beautiful face unmarred by traces of tears and remorse, her gentle manners unchanged. She talked pleasantly to all who came to visit, and she graced the drawing and dining rooms with her presence.

Only her belly continued to swell.

Some of the guests glanced at her stomach but said nothing. And some tried to refrain from looking, focusing their stares on her handsome forehead, her beautiful large hands, her light hair. And she rewarded them by smiling at them kindly with her gray eyes. She was faultless.

Only her belly continued to swell.

Her kind relatives considered the situation and resolved to send her to Vienna, where she would be a companion to their friend's childless wife.

She endeared herself to all.

And when she strolled in the street, large, quiet, and fair, she appeared regal. And when she sat in one of the cafés, the hem of her flowing dresses would fill the balcony around her. And the gentlemen who passed by stopped to tip their hats to her. She was treated gallantly.

Years passed, as in a slow-moving dream.

And those very years passed upon her son, upon Efrem, like a chain of punishments, expulsions, flights, and detentions.

Out of schools and back.

Oh, Efrem. The pitiful one, the wild. Without a father to rejoice in him and with a mother, a mother who knew not sorrow. Forever quiet and stately and beautiful, radiating dignity all about her.

So much so, that her son, too, respected her. And that very respect had become a part of himself.

And so, when they came to the Holy Land to live with their relatives in the American Colony, people began calling him by his mother's name, son of Ingmar. And deep in their hearts they nicknamed him, viciously, The Bastard.

Efrem wandered the streets and seemed to be reading their sinister thoughts, to be breathing their hissing speculations, to be sucking their venomous whispers, swallowing their hidden suspicions.

Tortured, he roamed the alleys and passageways of the city, and his love for his mother was great and hopeless.

He used to carry her bags to the hospital in the city where she cared for the sick. And he also accompanied her on her charitable visits to the homes of the poor. And as they walked along together, he supported her arm most courteously, and they talked.

She did not seem to chide him, nor complain nor offer him a string of compliments. They simply talked to each other.

Some said that French was spoken between them. What could they be talking about? Books? Music, perhaps?

When they passed, she, in her flowing skirts, radiated a cosmopolitan air.

And he walked her to the street corner, to the hospital gate, to the door of some unfortunate soul. No sooner had she disappeared than he darted forward. He dashed to his uncle's shop, or to the Colony's courtyard, or to the harness-maker's deserted hut at the edge of the valley at Bir Ayyub. Or he simply broke into an abandoned laughter. And then one day he went down to the foot of the Mount of Olives, at the eastern end of the valley. And he remained there.

Every now and then Yosef went there to help him heap the coals into the furnace and to carry the heavy copper and iron kettles across the yard.

And it was there that Yosef went after leaving the monastery on the day Um Ibrahim died. He gathered some twigs and bits of wood on his way, planning to make a fire and cook some coffee for Efrem and himself. But on that very day, one of the Arabs from the village of Siloam was bitten by a snake.

The village and valley were still resounding with ear-splitting cries when they sent out for Yosef.

Yosef remembered that Galen the Physician had taught his pupils to place suction cups on the area of the bite. Such is the rat, which, when bitten by a snake or a scorpion, rolls among the thorns and spines so that its skin gets pricked in as many places as possible, and the poison drains out through the holes.

Yosef hurried to the cave at the mountain's slope, where some years earlier he had hidden suction cups along with some jars and bottles. Where could he have put them? In the corner, among the rest of the American's forgotten articles, there lay a large gray wooden box, with two metal handles. Could they be in there?

Yosef blew the dust off the box, raised its lid, and lo, the box was filled with thick glass plates. For some reason, he picked one and raised it against the cave's opening. As he held it in his hand, the light of the valley streamed from behind the glass.

And against the light, and through the slide, looking down at him very clearly, was the double gate, the sealed one. Yes, that very gate! Those arched twins of a gazelle. Yes, yes! The Golden Gate—the Gate of Mercy.

How strange.

His hand eagerly drew another plate. There she was! The church of the Muscovites, unfinished still, as she was then—nestled against the mountain slope.

What marvelous glass plates. But the cries of the victim filled the air of the valley, urging him to go.

He searched the cave further and found the suction cups and rushed to the house of the afflicted man. He attended to him as best he could, then turned to go back to Efrem, who was still waiting for him at the doorway of the shack. But he was haunted by the lingering memory of the victim's cry.

Why did Hezekiah the king see fit to crush the copper serpent? The sages were grateful to him for having done so.

No wonder—since then many snakes had broken away from their masters. *And they were now in the steep ravines, and in the clefts of the rocks, and on all the thorn bushes, and in all the pastures.* The snake. In all his seven names: cobra, echis, serpent, viper, basilisk, cerastes, adder.

Today of all days, Yosef, today it would seem most appropriate to add another charm to ward off the snake. To add it to the one already carved into your belt. Over there, on the path leading to the valley, camel caravans used to pass. And sometimes, during the month of Ramadan, the valley was covered with a multitude of camels, the young camels of Midian and Efah. And also a caravan of Ishmaelites from Gilead, going down to Egypt.

And the caravans left behind them colored glass beads that had fallen off the camels' necks. The beads were strewn all over the path. And so, as he sat on the ground telling Efrem son of Ingmar slowly, and with a stammer, all about the days before he had come with his father to the holy city, he was stringing blue beads he had collected on his way.

And he also told him about the American who had stayed at the inn in the American Colony and about the days of his illness in the cave, until the day he was last seen in the courtyard of the railway station. And he was never again heard from in Jerusalem.

By then Yosef had finished working on the beads and the belt. And right beside the inscription, *Dan shall be a serpent,* there was embroidered in blue beads: *Yosef is a fruitful bough, a fruitful bough by a spring.* And it is written in the Talmud: Read not "by a spring," but "above the power of the evil eye." For in the Hebrew *alei ayn*—by the spring—could be read *olei ayn*—over the evil eye. And thus he was safe from the power of the evil eye.

And so Yosef girded his amended belt around his waist and climbed, reassured, the path leading to the village. It was a lovely day in the month of Tishrei, and his vigorous steps rose high, high. *Raise a song: Sing aloud to God our strength, shout for joy to the God of Jacob. Sound the timbrel, the sweet lyre with the harp.*

The month of Tishrei.

Yes, Yehosef, and tomorrow, the tenth of the month.

Tomorrow is Yom Kippur . . .

*And then up the camel caravan path, all strewn with colorful glass beads.*

*O*n that Yom Kippur the synagogue at Brandeis was filled to capacity. It was a lovely Tishrei day. A beautiful autumn day. A Boston autumn day. And through the windows, the green hills of Boston were rising.

What had come over them on that day? Why were they so burdened? Were they about to burst? A portentous day.

And by noon the bad news had already come rolling in like a storm. Bad news. My anguish, my anguish! For I heard the sound of the shofar, the alarm of war. And then the radio and television sets began carrying the horror. By morning it would be all over. By morning. Or perhaps by nightfall. There was only terror in trying to comprehend the news. And the news was bad. The war looked bad. What was happening? Had the Lord risen up as on Mount Perazim to do His deed? Strange was His deed! Had He really planned to gather all the multitude of nations that fight against Ariel?

Had "that day" really come, and had the Lord, as on

*Until the day he was last seen in the courtyard of the railway station. And he was never again heard from in Jerusalem.*

[ 79 ]

Mount Perazim, risen up to do His deed, and His feet stood on the Mount of Olives, and the mountain was split in two?!

What had happened to the mountains?

Gaping, ravenous, they could not be satisfied. What did the mountains ask for?

What did they want?

Do you not know? Do you not know what they are asking? Don't you?

Yes, *to offer a sacrifice there an everlasting statute upon one of the mountains, to make atonement for the house of Israel.*

I pray Thee, let it be, only this once, just one burnt offering, one unblemished sacrifice—will it make atonement for all the sons? Once—and let the mountains rest. Satisfied. Appeased. Forever?

And on the third day, from afar:

"Whom should we send? Who will become the offering?"

"*God will provide himself the lamb. For a burnt-offering, my son.*"

Yosef, my son—

Yosef, my lad, will you forgive me?

*A*nd Haya, Hacham Nehunia's wife, realized that Yosef had failed to come for his bread both that day and the day before, and a lump of cold fear settled within her heart, pressing upon and gnawing at the walls of her womb. She held back her groan, and her eyelids were shrouded in shadow.

She sent to look for him.

He could not be found. Neither in his father's house nor in all the houses of the sick. He could not be found. She sent for her husband at the synagogue. Let them all look for him.

They looked for him upon the mountains!

And in the evening they found him, slain.

A bullet from a Turkish gun was lodged in his neck, his blood spilled on the ground.

When the news of Yosef reached the courtyard at the American Colony, Sophie daughter of Ingmar asked that a mule be hitched to a cart so that she might go to the valley, to Bir Ayyub. The boy, one of the Colony's youths, led her down there. He tied the reins to a tree trunk and sat on the ground to wait for her.

She alighted, tall and fair, the brim of her hat hiding half her still-beautiful face, and she walked slowly toward the shack.

Her appearance caused a sudden hush among the cackling, prattling flock of village women. Efrem, who was bent over the furnace and blowing the coals with the bellows, heard the sudden silence and abruptly turned around.

He saw his mother's large frame coming toward him, the circle of stillness around her growing wider, rippling. Efrem straightened his glistening, perspiring body. With one hand he fixed the headband that kept his dark, unruly hair off his forehead; with the other he waved away the simple women who remained standing there, pushing each other.

Sophie was coming closer, and behind her were all the grays and purples of the horizon, as though her presence filled the entire valley.

Efrem stood there, motionless, a strange sigh of relief stirring at the base of his throat. The horrible premonition that had loomed over him since that morning finally came down like a cloud. It came down and swaddled his heart. Mother was here now. She put her arm through his bare one, and immediately her sleeve and the side of her dress turned yellow and gray as they soaked up his perspiration.

Would he walk her to the shaded corner at the crossroads by Hakal Dama? It was cool there. They could sit down and rest. Did he wonder what had brought her there? Something strange. But lovely.

*At the crossroads by Hakal Dama.*

She had had a dream.

And in her dream Malachi, the last of the prophets, came to see her. He sat beside her with a sigh. "And 'Sophie,' he said, 'Sophie, I have one more chapter, but I resolved not to write it. How could I have written it, Sophie, and given it to the people? For they are bewildered and frightened, embittered and harried, all of them. They are persecuted and weary, lost and forsaken, bound and forlorn.

"'How could I have written it?

"'Until you came along, Sophie. Come, let me explain the last chapter to you.

"'Our Father in heaven created man, in His image He created him. An image, He created Him. His own image, His own reflection. An image of fatherhood. Man, unto father was born . . .'

"Is it not so, Efrem? Is this not the way of every man? Does not every man have a father? A father who has begotten him? A father who loves him? Who saves him and protects him and teaches him his ways and guides him? Who shows him the righteous path. . . .

"'And he, the father, calls his son to him before his death, and he makes a will. And what does he bequeath him? All that he has taught him, all that he has shown him, the path that the son should choose: This is his will.

"'And the son, once the father dies, has a father no more.

"'This is the way of every man.

"'And man in the image of God was created. In His

image, His reflection. An image of fatherhood, of our Father in Heaven. Who created the universe, and put His people there, and gave them His Law, His legacy, and the prophets—and died. And all we have left of Him is His will and testament, to guard us, to comfort us, to guide us in the right path.

"'And there is no life in the world to come
And the resurrection of the dead is none
And there is no messiah
And there is no savior
And the kingdom of God is not near at all
And there is neither Eden, nor Sheol.

"'Only the road, the road alone is the source of re-demption, the spring of rest, the bequest, the fountain of peace. And of freedom.'

"Thus spoke to me the prophet Malachi. And it can all be found in the fourth chapter, which was not written. And beyond that, there is nothing. And this is the way of every man."

So said Sophie daughter of Ingmar to Efrem.

How did she say it? In Swedish? Or perhaps in French?

And Efrem stood there, transfixed, and the cold cloud was spreading from his heart down to his innards, to his groin.

Sending heavy waves to the tips of his toes.

Had she come all the way from the Colony to tell him about her strange dream?

To add a chapter to the Book of the Prophet Malachi?
Or?

Or? No! No!

"Mother, Mother, Mother!? Who is it?"

"A friend, Efrem, a friend."

"Which one, Mother?" And he quickly went over the short list.

"Yakub? He's been sick."

"No, it is not Yakub."

"Torkilad?"

"No, it is not Torkilad."

"Mother!? Who, then? Tomas?"

And he went on counting, and the circle was coming to a close.

And then his eyes read, they read wildly the name that was coming out of her lips.

"Yosef? Why Yosef?"

And a chant from an ancient lamentation spilled out of his heart:

"Why Yo-o-o-sef?"

And when he leaped forward, he seemed to chase after the echo that was wailing upon the mountains, toward the village of Siloam.

And in the village, Nehunia's wife covered her face, and no one spoke to her. For they saw how great was her grief. Nor did they let her join the funeral procession. She was with child.

She did not follow his coffin, nor did she see the site of his grave. She sat in mourning for many days, weeping in secret. And tear-drenched days were followed by dream-tortured nights.

Haya, listen to me, do not refuse to be comforted.

The days would steal away like a dream. They would rush past like a cloud, and even the heart so bruised in pain, the heart, too, would cradle itself inside the grief, and slowly, slowly, wrapped like an etrog in the month of Tishrei, it would cuddle itself, swaddle itself in a soft down of sweet sorrow.

Do not refuse to be comforted. Soon *a spring day will come, and cyclamen will bloom, and the mountains and the valleys will be covered with red anemones.* You will be able to visit Yosef's grave. To weep for him, for fair Yosef. For he is dead.

Even Efrem's savage pain would subside slowly.

On the day of the burial Efrem was brought back to the Colony, sick and delirious.

He lay in his mother's room for several days. He shivered feverishly, feeling as though he were being skinned alive. A ray of light, a creaking door, the call of the rooster, all sent twisted waves of pain through his body.

And on the third day, still feverish and hallucinating, he felt as though he were being carried to the mountain, to Yosef's burial site.

And over there, instead of a tombstone, Yosef was rising, sprouting from his grave. He was buried from the waist down, but from his loins—he sprouted. And as he looked at Efrem with his half-closed, bright yellow eyes, Yosef was blooming.

Efrem did not know then that the vision would visit him every year in the spring, at the beginning of the month of Nissan. That he would dream the dream of Yosef rising and sprouting from his grave, smiling at him from his crown, a magnificently mocking smile. Yosef's smile.

Smiling, he would look through him and beyond him into the valley, to the point where the rambling city wall extends southward, into the heart of the King's Garden, with its lovely fruit-laden trees. And on to the tree of the prophet Isaiah by the mound of stones, in Ein Rogel. Is it a mulberry tree?

Or a carob? Some say an oak.

And from there down to Hakal Dama and the railway station. And then up the camel caravan path, all strewn with colorful glass beads.

And he would look at his beloved Kidron Valley, just as it was captured in those glass plates. In those slides.

Efrem, Efrem, you have got to do something about those slides!

You must not leave them for months and years to lie in the corner of some cave, like stones unturned! You must get hold of that gray box once and for all and take it to the photographer's shop next to the American Colony.

And those diligent photographers will develop them into lovely pictures on large squares of glossy paper. . . .

*And his beloved Kidron Valley.*

But Efrem was still shivering feverishly. His illness was slow to subside, and when he finally recovered from that strange fever, he was weak and jumpy. Only slowly did he begin to gather strength and to walk on his own.

Perhaps he could even make it to that cave at the mountain slope.

And so it happened that one day Edward showed the box of slides to his friend Arthur, an amateur photographer. Arthur got very excited and decided right then and there to develop them into pictures on large squares of glossy paper.

No sooner said than done.

And as Edward stood in Arthur's darkroom in the basement of his house, seeing the pictures for the first time, he was forever robbed of his peace of mind. For weeks he sent letters to all whom the matter might concern, as well as to those in charge of his affairs in Boston. He closed his business in the city, and in the month of Nissan we boarded an El Al plane bound for Israel.

*And his beloved Kidron Valley.*

*I*n the morning, I had a cup of coffee at Café Savion in Rehavia, and afterwards—"Greta," in a white dress and wide-brimmed hat—made my way toward old Mr. Stein's book store.

Ay, ay, ay, old Mr. Stein, I was playing Greta games on you, and it worked. Just as it worked on Ernst years before. For Ernst, I had been Brünn in the days prior to World War I. I was Czechoslovakia. And it also worked on the late Professor Benedict. For him, too, I was the world of yesteryear.

It was not intentional. I truly had not planned it. It was all so very simple. They were the directors; I, the player. And now, again, in white dress and white hat covering half my face. Quietly.

It was quiet in the store. I wandered about, softly, resonating the world of yesterday. First, let the rest of the customers leave, and only afterwards: "Good day, Mr. Stein. I am looking for a book on Jerusalem by that eccentric old lady from the American Colony."

He did not have it. But he would look for it. In the meantime, would Madame care to look at *Jerusalem,* by Selma Lagerlöf?

His eyes were shining.

His daily worries were peeling off. There was a spark

in his darting eyes. He seemed pleased. Greta and Stefan Zweig for five pleasant minutes in Jerusalem of 1974.

Would Madame come back on Sunday?

I came back on Monday. In a violet suit. For a moment, he did not recognize me.

"Yes, Madame?"

Greta was weaving quiet, slowness, tranquility, and yesterday.

I smiled.

The spark was rekindled in old Mr. Stein's eye. And there was no need to bow or to kiss my hand. It was all there, in his happy smile. Yes, he had looked into the matter of that eccentric old lady's book. He had not forgotten.

There was nothing he could report as yet. Would Madame care to come back once more?

Once more? What a silly old gentleman! Once, twice, and even a third time. The whole thing was like balm to my bones. It felt so pleasant that as I walked down the streets of Rehavia, my feet hardly touched the ground. I was growing taller, and my legs were getting longer. A certain happiness flowed into me from the sidewalks, filling me with Wonderland's delight.

Yes, he would look into the matter of the book for my sake, mine alone, Greta, Queen of Jerusalem.

Ah, the days of Nissan in Rehavia are lovely.

But it was necessary to travel to the American Colony Hotel in East Jerusalem to try and get an interview with its owner, Mr. Horatio Spafford-Vester, a descendant of the founding family. Once again, then, in a white, wide-brimmed hat and a white dress. Should I try to replay the world of yesteryear for Mr. Vester?

Would he be charmed?

The taxi, driven by an Arab driver, brought me to the entrance of the hotel garden. It was a brilliant morning, and the veiled garden, captive in her dream, had nothing to do but shade the birds that were singing among the boughs.

Not a guest to be seen.

I came out of the taxi slowly, heading straight into Mr. Vester's arms. Almost.

For there he was, standing at the entrance to the garden, with his sagging pink cheeks, his British look, and his mouth, which seemed nothing more than a thin lip line, very straight.

Scene I: Splendid! I would make a grand entrance. I would get out of the car, move confidently toward him, and say: "Mr. Vester, I presume?"

Only at that very moment my purse got stuck in the seat of the car. I was still struggling to rescue it when three Arab workers approached him and took him away. They were building a new fence in the Colony's courtyard and needed his advice.

Thus Mr. Vester was dropped from the scene of my grand entrance. And I remained there for a moment, a foolish woman at the tail end of her girlhood, clad in white. I was standing on the cool tiles of the hotel lobby, with only a clerk to talk to.

"I have come from Boston, Massachusetts, and I am interested in the history of the American Colony. Could you kindly arrange an interview for me with the owners?"

He made a phone call.

And I remained standing in the lobby until Mr. Vester showed up.

He was a tough sort. He had already been told on the phone that I was a Goldberg. True, I had said, "Dr. Goldberg," and that bleary-eyed clerk repeated my title, but as Mr. Vester made his way toward me I was nothing more to him than, "Mrs. Goldberg, no?"

Mrs. And a Goldberg.

That was it. Everything was over and done with. The Goldberg had popped up and attached itself to my white garb, fastened itself like a kitchen apron, and would not come off.

End of Scene I: Cut!

Mr. Vester asked me to wait for him for about twenty minutes. He would be back.

So be it. I would prepare the setting for the next scene.

In the hotel garden, beneath a giant cypress, beside a small marble-top table shaded by a blue umbrella, I ordered a glass of red wine.

How beautiful was the red inside the glass on the marble top. The morning light had deepened it so, that antique red. The garden was deserted, and in it was a lemon tree laden with fruit, and a tall palm. There were also well-tended square flower beds, and pots filled with geraniums, on the ground and on the balconies. And in the center of the tiled courtyard was a small fish pond. The red wine was playing on the marble surface.

Nu, Mr. Vester?

Mr. Vester was taking his time, and the game was beginning to lose its flavor. There was no one in the garden besides me. Not one guest.

Let's see now: In which of these rooms might Efrem son of Ingmar have lain during those late Nissan days? Shivering feverishly until, little by little, his illness subsided, and he pulled himself together and got out of bed, weak and jumpy. It was a strange fever. And during those days, another guest had joined the Colony's courtyard and became one of its residents.

*E*ver since he stumbled upon the group of forsaken, destitute, and famished Yemenites, the founder of the American Colony had arranged that its residents set up a special fund to aid them. And so, even after their brethren, the notables of Jerusalem, had offered to help them, the Yemenites continued to come to the Colony's courtyard for their allocations.

That is, until they became self-supporting. As soon as they found some employment, as, for example, maintenance men at the opulent households of the city, they went up to the Colony and notified their benefactors that they no longer needed their generous charity.

The Colony's residents greatly respected those wiry "members of the tribe of Gad." They viewed them as noble and dignified people who never asked for more than their bare necessities, and who never took more than they needed for a modest existence.

Among these Yemenites was old Levi, Yosef's father.

Levi, like his father before him, was a *shohet,* a ritual slaughterer.

Ah, those tranquil Thursdays of long ago. How he held that chicken in his hands, the one he had snatched from the owner. He held it under his arm, the fingers of his left hand clasping its comb, pulling its head backwards so that its neck was well stretched while its legs were parted.

Then, with the fingers of his right hand he plucked the neck feathers once or twice, while little Yosef, sitting at his feet, watched him murmur the blessing. He watched as it all happened at once: a pass of the sharp knife; another tug of the comb; the dark thick blood spilling on the ground; and his father's shoe raking the dirt to cover it. Then his father tossed the slaughtered chicken to the ground away from him. It fidgeted about, its bloody head hung loosely to one side, dragging behind as the chicken continued to struggle. Didn't it know it had been killed? One more convulsion, one more jerky move, and it fell silent, its eyes, in death as in life—stupid yellow glass beads.

His father stood beneath the castor-oil tree, wiping his knife clean with one of the wide leaves.

Over here, in the village of Siloam, no one needed

his craft. In their poverty, the Yemenites had no chickens to kill.

And so, old Levi no longer needed his gray whetstone, whose center was concave from use. It was orphaned on the day he found a job as the groundskeeper at the courtyard of one of the notables of Jerusalem. Who knows how long it would have lain like a stone unturned if it were not for little Yosef, who had picked it up and hidden it in his shirt pocket, and guarded it as he would a precious gem.

On the day old Levi was appointed groundskeeper of Señor Meyuhas's garden, he walked up to the Colony, presented himself before his benefactors, and made an announcement. With the help of God, blessed be His name, he had found a source of income. He would no longer need their charitable allocations. He was now the groundskeeper at Señor Meyuhas's, where he weeded the gardens, cleared the stones, pine needles, and casuarina leaves from the square flower beds, and watered the geranium plants in the pots around the yard.

Señor Meyuhas had three daughters, all sweet-spoken and fluent in French. And all three charmed their father with their words, chirping and cooing, until he granted their wish and agreed to have a pipe, the likes of which had never been seen in the courtyards of Jerusalem, installed in their house.

And this is the story of that pipe:

Señor Meyuhas's wife and daughters consulted among themselves and hired a plumber who installed a metal pipe that carried water from the cistern in the yard into the washroom inside the house. The pipe climbed into the house through a small hole in the wall, and once inside, its head was bent over a large, gleaming copper tub that stood in the center of the washroom.

If a man stood next to the water-hole, hung the pipe over a pulley made especially for it, and began to pump, the water would flow up, gurgling at first, finally pouring coolly and pleasantly into the tub.

So it happened that old Levi became the water-pipe attendant. He stood there throughout the spring and summer, pumping the water, until the last of the affluent gentleman's daughters peeped through the window and yelled out that the bathing was finished.

So passed many lovely spring and summer days, until that day in the month of Tishrei when Yosef was found slain on the mountain.

While Yosef, his son, was still alive, old Levi could not speak to him peaceably. But the day the news of his son's death reached him, it seemed that the springs of his lean life had run dry. He could not touch food nor drink, and the neighbors' pleas and entreaties were of no avail; nor were the rabbi's threats. Finally an elderly widow, one of those supported by the American Colony, dragged her feet uptown and presented herself to Sophie daughter of Ingmar.

With the help of the son of the apostate, who was fluent in the tongues of the East and West, the woman related the saga of old Levi, who was fast shriveling up in his grief. Sophie daughter of Ingmar listened and had him brought over to the Colony's courtyard. It was there that he remained till the end of his days—a mute, shrunken resident. He weeded the small vegetable gardens behind the kitchen, carried the peels to the stables, and swept the stone tiles clean with a wicker broom.

Aha! The position of groundskeeper and pump attendant at Señor Meyuhas's courtyard had been vacated! Who would fill it?

Who would fill it?

There was Efrem son of Ingmar. Bony and emaciated after his illness, he never returned to his shack in the valley. He drifted.

Tortured and melancholic, he wandered about the city. He returned to the Colony only at dusk, much to the concern of his uncle Olaf and his friends, all fathers of growing daughters.

$A$nd so his wandering took him westward, to the Jewish Quarter, to Mishkenot Yisrael, a neighborhood known for its lovely houses, at the end of which, shaded by a wall of cypresses, was the courtyard of the prominent silk merchant, Señor Meyuhas.

The heat of the sidewalk passed through his sandals, penetrated his feet, and flowed into his body. He brushed his hand over the cypress hedge that surrounded the courtyard. The branches swished against his fingers, and the sound was echoed by his sandals.

The street was deserted, except for the echo of his sandals. It was late in the afternoon, the hour when gently bred girls played Chopin etudes to the street through the closed shutters.

They were surely wearing neatly pressed white muslin dresses, the freshly mopped tile floors were still damp, and it was cool inside those rooms, beyond the closed shutters, beyond the fences, beyond envy.

On the following day, and on the next, Efrem found himself at the entrance to the courtyard, listening to the tunes, drinking in the music.

On the third day, he learned from the village woman carrying the fig baskets all about the house and the beauty of its daughters, and about the disappearance of the old groundskeeper who had been gone for many weeks.

So Efrem got himself hired to the post of gardener and guard of the silk merchant's courtyard.

Señor Meyuhas's house was lively, filled with song and laughter. Peddlers of all sorts, villagers carrying fresh produce, various emissaries and messengers—all paraded in and out throughout the morning. Those hours buzzed with activity, but by noontime silence had settled upon the house, which now slept and rested. Late in the afternoon, the balconies were spread open to the sounds of the evening—song and play and conversations among neighbors and guests, and the clinking of dainty cups. And there was the aroma of coffee and the fragrance of freshly baked pastry. And knitting needles were clicking softly over mint tea and preserves. A lively house.

The gentleman's daughters were well-bred young girls. Like most daughters of good families from Salonika, they, too, had dark eyes and thick brows, and a soft tuft of fine dark hair adorned their crimson lips. They were good-looking and laughed easily.

A lively house.

The oldest among them was exceedingly beautiful and bright. The firstborn, Luna, sunny and pure, was the jewel in her father's crown. Who could count her virtues?

Who could describe her beauty?

*He who desires to see Luna's beauty, let him take a goblet of pure silver, fill it with the kernels of a red pomegranate, encircle its brim with a wreath of red roses and set it between sun and shade—and the lustrous glow is akin to the beauty of Luna Meyuhas.*

Her face, under a mane of luxurious curly hair, was alabaster; her finely hewn forehead shimmered with childhood's majestic dew. She had a fine straight nose, and her mouth, with its graceful crimson lips, was the only one in the family not marked with the soft, downy tuft that adorned the lips of the girls of Salonika. Her eyebrows, too, were unlike her sisters'. They did not meet over the bridge of her nose, but were beautifully drawn over her marvelous eyes: the dark ones. And that untamed lioness' head towered over her delicate, white neck, over her slender shoulders. Her fine, gentle hands moved gracefully. She was altogether lovely, from head to waist.

From her waist down, she was heavy.

A certain heaviness gravitated from her toward the earth.

Or, from the earth toward her?

There was something terrifying in her heavy gait, which gravitated rhythmically to and from the earth, and in her laughter, which was not playful but seemed to bubble on its own, casting its spell over all who heard it. She ruled over the entire household; she was its crowned queen, the pride of her father.

Many tutors came to teach her. They came with books and with music, with canvases and brushes and water-colors. And they went.

They were the best. She drank their gifts and knowledge, languages, books and music, absorbing it all. Others replaced them, and she exhausted these as well. She was as astounded as they at how fast their wellsprings of knowledge dried up in her presence.

Her grandfather was beginning to worry about that laughter, which seemed to issue from her throat all on its own. And so he began to pay attention to hints dropped by the congregation's notables and their messengers concerning well-born, well-bred eligible young men.

But Luna turned a deaf ear. She was comfortable in her home and saw no reason to trade it for another. She wanted no part of either the best match or the noblest prospect.

Much to her grandfather's concern she had already shrugged off many a good match. Finally, he urged her mother to persuade her.

At the merciful hour of dusk, her mother revealed to her the secret of her own youth. She related the story of her brave love, whom her parents had banished from the city. And she told her how she had been forced by her parents to marry Señor Meyuhas from Salonika, that short, stout man, with a slight limp. How she had fainted on her wedding day right under the canopy, and how chaos had ensued among the guests. How her father—Luna's grandfather—picked up a bucket of water standing nearby, dumped it over her head, and helped her back to her feet. And as he was supporting her, he motioned to the rabbi, who signaled the groom to proceed with the wedding vows. And so she was wed according to the Law. And how he, Señor Meyuhas, tried to please her, to appease her, plying her with gifts and sweets. And before too many years had passed, the sound of her own laughter had joined that of the rest of the house.

A lively house. A lively house.

Luna looked at her mother in bewilderment. Had she, Luna, asked for a husband? Had she yearned for a lively house when the whole world outside lay before her, and who knows what wonders it might hold?

For Luna's wells and fountains burst forth only from her mind. Only her mind longed to conquer and be conquered. And they, all of them, failed to see and understand.

That is, except for her grandfather, who saw and understood and muttered to himself: "Erudite women bear no children." In his heart he called her bright, alabaster forehead "a brazen forehead," and deep down he had a sense of foreboding.

On the day Efrem got himself hired as groundskeeper at Señor Meyuhas's courtyard, he also inherited old Levi's post at the water pump. And from that day on, the water that had flowed in a cool pleasant stream burst forth in a heated gush. And it whistled as it splashed, hardening nipples and raising breasts, flash flooding backs, until it dissolved into a delightful titillation.

And Luna, like her two younger sisters, found herself waiting for the hour when the gravel path was trampled under the Swede's agile steps. And as she stood under the cold water salvo, she laughed playfully as she heard the fragments of that dark, abandoned laughter coming her way through the stone wall.

One day, while propping the pipe over the pulley, Efrem broke it. He put it down and walked toward the house. He stopped at the entrance and knocked on the door.

Luna opened it.

He was lean, tall, tanned, and young. The skin over his handsome high cheekbones was taut, his deep-set black eyes were "blazing." Just as in the novels about gypsies.

He stood proudly at the door. A prince!

And he conquered her with his look. For the first time in her life her eyes met a man's—a real man.

What more did she need to get up and follow him? Her mother used to sing in a voice filled with longing:

When I was sixteen
innocent and green
I fell in love
with a cunning gypsy. . . .

Except that the knocking on the door had reached her grandfather's ears as well.

He, too, saw that dark and handsome vagabond at the door.

Ridden with worry, he reached a decision.

A firm one.

On that very day he swore that he would go to see every prominent man in the city, east and west, and plead with him. He would not hold back any gift nor excuse, until he succeeded in getting that dark demon out of the city.

And he did.

On the following morning, accompanied by the imposing figure of the community's rabbi, Luna's grandfather traveled east in a coach hitched to two fine-looking horses. When they reached the workshop of Olaf son of Ingmar, they stopped.

Olaf received the dignified guests with due respect, offered them coffee, and sent for two of the Colony's elders. An hour later, the old gentleman emerged from the workshop, followed by the other four. They all appeared pleased and optimistic.

That evening, they summoned Efrem to the workshop. He was notified that he had been chosen to carry out a task of utmost importance, that he would be well paid, and that by the end of the month he would have to board a ship that was sailing to London. From there he would continue on his way to Boston, Massachusetts, in America. Efrem stood there stalling, listening to their pregnant silence, playing a small game of revenge on them. He delayed his answer for a very long time. Finally, and very slowly, he nodded his head in defiant agreement, as if saying: Go I will, for what have I got to lose?

But inside his bony rib cage his heart quivered. Boston? Did they say Boston, Massachusetts? Wasn't Boston the native city of the unfortunate American, the one he had heard about on that bitter day in the valley, by the shack?

He must leave that room slowly and proudly. Then he could turn and run to the Kidron Valley, to search the cave in the mountain slope.

The box! Was it still there?

Efrem dashed forward, climbed the mountain and disappeared inside its belly, went in and out, until he erupted from one of the caves, cradling a long, gray wooden box in his arms.

Very thirsty, he gulped the entire breadth of the valley with agile strides. He climbed the mountain on the opposite side, where, at the top, a family of nomads had built a temporary café. That was his destination.

It was the end of autumn, and of the century.

As he moved closer to the makeshift café, he came across a group of Swedish tourists.

Among them, on top of the mountain, at the threshold of the twentieth century, comely as Jerusalem, stood the writer Selma Lagerlöf.

She stood there, drinking in the entire city with her wise, knowing eyes.

Years later she would write a book. And she would

*On top of the mountain, across the way, a family of nomads had built a makeshift café.*

call it *Jerusalem,* and she would attain everlasting fame.

And thus, between one century and another, Efrem met the illustrious Selma Lagerlöf.

Selma, in Celtic, means the one who is fair,
but Shalem, in Hebrew, is Jerusalem.
Did Selma know, was she aware
that the capital's name
she had come to bear?

That evening, dusty and tired, Efrem stood at the door of the photographer's studio near the American Colony, holding the long, gray wooden box by its metal handles.

The shadows spread over the hotel's garden. Why was Mr. Vester so long in coming? The wine in the glass had receded and reached the bottom. Had I been a famous writer, rich or beautiful, would he have left me waiting like that? In the hotel's shaded garden? The shaded garden, dreaming, was watching the palm tree rising from her navel. And a giant cypress was breathing there, and there was a lemon tree amidst the square flowerbeds.

At that hour, hidden in the bower, fair, serene, and silent.

The garden swooned, tranquil and warm, sleeping away the afternoon, no one knowing her heart.

And my heart was wrapped in sadness.

*Did I grieve over the beauty of her humble world,*
*Its bright dreams, crystal visions?*

*Or over all my secret reveries? My many visions, those*
*foundlings of my heart, of which I brood day and night?*

But it was all in vain. All in vain.

"Waiter! Another glass, and . . . kindly, an ice cube, if you please?"

"An ice cube? In red wine!"

He groaned disdainfully, and I shrank into nothingness before his eyes.

"Yes. Yes, an ice cube. And in red wine, if you please."

Just you wait. Wait until the day my name attains world fame. Then you will come to understand that the ways of acclaimed authors are often different, unlike most people's. The day will come when you, still a petty waiter, will relish the memory of those late afternoon hours when, on a marble table-top, you placed before me a glass of red wine with an ice cube. Yes.

Mr. Vester was slow to come.

What have I to do with you all? True, I am not one of the famous authors, neither am I a woman of riches, prominence, or great beauty. But I am the daughter of kings, and my ancestors reigned in Jerusalem in the days of Hezekiah!

Moreover, Mr. Vester, you may have a lemon tree in your courtyard, but in my garden there grows an etrog! And . . .

And Mr. Vester returned. He sat down beside me most courteously, ordered himself a glass of red wine—without an ice cube—and listened to me politely. Afterwards, coolly gallant and joyless, he showed me around the Colony and recounted its history for the umpteenth time. He glanced at my pictures with reserved kindness, remarking that he had a sister who lived in the city and was most knowledgeable about its pathways and history.

Mr. Vester's sister sat in her office at the Family and Children's Clinic in East Jerusalem. The clinic had been founded by her great-grandmother, one of the first settlers of the Colony, and now she was its director. She was an attractive woman, pleasant, outgoing, and clever. And it was she who, at the end of that visit, placed a small cardboard box in my arms.

*From the days of the Jewish settlers in the Sharon.*

A small square box containing, yes, old slides. Of glass.

"From the days of the Jewish settlers in the Sharon," was what she said. She was cleaning her drawers one day and found the slides there. She would entrust them to me if I cared to have them.

And so, in the reception room of the Family and Children's Clinic in East Jerusalem, a small box of slides was delivered unto me, on my lap.

And I asked myself: Who has begotten these? It was none other than my own box of slides that had borne them, to be placed in my arms and under my care!

I felt faint. There was no end to it. The photographs were flooding my life. I had to get up and flee. And the pleasant, understanding voice of the director followed me to the door:

"They used to have quite a few pictures and prints over at the studio next to the Colony. They may still have them stashed away somewhere in their back room."

Do they have old ones, first of their kind like mine? I wondered.

"Taxi! To the souvenir shop next to the American Colony Hotel, please."

It was still open.

Inside the store my hands lightly touched scarves and pieces of embroidered fabrics; they stroked the necks of wooden camels and donkeys, and they brushed over postcards of dried flowers and bowls filled with hand-blown green glass beads. And, as I've said before, I can never walk out of a store empty-handed. I have always been terrified of storekeepers. And so I bought myself a small, silly-looking camel caravan carved of olive wood and covered with a sticky layer of resin. And I also bought a mother-of-pearl necklace. And as I stood there, fingering the white beads innocently, I quietly removed the tiny silver cross that was attached to the necklace and let it drop softly on the pile of embroidered fabrics. And I turned to the young salesman:

"Do you happen to have any pictures left of the kind they used to sell as souvenirs from the Holy Land?" I asked him pleasantly.

"Yes, Madame. They are in the box in the corner over there. They are not in very good order," he apologized.

For the second time that afternoon I felt faint.

Standing in the corner, somewhat deceptively, was a box filled with pictures. My hands rummaged among them weakly. Some were old, some new. There was no end to it.

No end to it. I had decreed it upon myself. The waves of photographs and their tides were rising against me, about to flood my life.

And what if there were among them old ones, one-of-a-kind ones, like mine? I was overtaken by a strange jealousy.

I had no choice but to buy them. The whole box. I would buy it and be off. And back home, in Boston, I would hide it in the attic where no one could see it.

"I'll buy the box. The whole box."

And the lad, the young, smooth Armenian salesman, stood over me, grinning.

What's the matter, my sweet young man? Why are you standing smiling like this? But his hesitant eyes, with the beautiful lashes, avoided mine.

One moment, please. Just let me leave the store. Please . . .

But it was too late. I had already had a glimpse of his eyes, which were steeped in the sorrows of his people.

I had been struck . . .

And so, once Efrem had decided to take the box of slides to Boston, he took them to the photographer's studio. He brought them over to the Armenian lad who apprenticed there, so that he would develop them into pictures on large squares of glossy paper.

The studio was empty, except for Sahik Doukhourian, who stood there examining his beautiful, delicate hands.

They were long and slender, and his straight fingers were intertwined with delicate veins. Only the nails, arched and long, were blackened at the tips from film processing.

When Efrem entered the studio and threw the box on top of the counter, Sahik recoiled and blinked his lovely, long-lashed eyes to the rattling sound of the glass in the box.

"Open!" Efrem snarled.

Sahik raised his graceful hands. He rubbed one with the other delicately and then, as if touching some contemptible creature, he undid the metal hook on the cover of the box and rubbed his hands once again. Afterwards, with only his thumb and index finger, and most reservedly, he pulled out a single slide. And with an agile move of his right hand he passed the slide to his left, and wiped the right on his sweater. He raised the slide toward the shop entrance.

And there, against the light, looking at him very clearly, was the tower of Abu Khasem, on the mountain near Gethsemane.

How strange.

The mountain was bold. The onion-domed church of Maria Magdalena was not there! It had not yet been built! The Abu Khasem tower alone was rising there. Protruding. The mountain's only sovereign.

"Old slides, first of their kind. There are no others like them!" With a flourish he pointed to the box: "No others like them."

"Print them, then. On large squares of glossy paper. By the end of this month!" Efrem son of Ingmar commanded in English, and left the store.

Alone at last, Sahik Doukhourian drew out the rest of the slides. He held them against the light, one after the other, between his thumb and index finger, his long lashes fluttering at the lovely sights that looked down at him. There were no others like them! They had no peer. And how beautiful they were! And who knows, they might be most valuable. Who knows? And suppose some accidentally dropped into his desk drawer and remained hidden there—who would know about it? It was well known by then that by the end of that month, Efrem son of Ingmar was to sail across the oceans. And . . .

And so it happened that on the appointed day Efrem appeared in the store. He moved his eyes from the prints to the slides and back again and gave him, Sahik, a terrible smile. He bared his gleaming white teeth at him. And he gave him his mocking, bitter smile.

The Armenian lad was very frightened.

He began rummaging in his desk drawer with trembling hands. His nostrils paled and widened, and a frightful weariness settled into his legs, a heavy weariness, just like in those long hours in his childhood when he had stood, an orphan, among the choir boys during services. They stood there forever. To the point of tears and despair.

*How strange. The mountain was bold. The onion-domed church of Maria Magdalena was not there! Not yet built! The Abu Khasem tower alone was rising there. . . .*

Sahik Doukhourian.

Poor, poor Sahik. Why have I conjured you up to trouble me, and what should I do with you now?

Will you, too, hang about me, restless and haunted?

Sahik, listen to me. No one will find out about the missing slides. I, too, have already forgiven you. Did you believe for a moment that I would punish you for your little transgression? For that little sin you committed before our eyes?

Relax, Sahik, rest again quietly. No one will know about it. Not even Efrem. He was just standing there smiling his bitter smile at you. He knew nothing of the few missing slides, Sahik.

Sahik? Sahik, listen to me!

But in his fear and desperation, Sahik had already lost his senses.

Oh, tormented brother!

One in whose memory were embedded the shadows of his ravaged parents, the moans of his slain brothers, all of the tears of his people and the misery of his own heart. They all existed there, a merciless mass of horror. And then, a shaven-headed orphan, he was taken to the Armenian Quarter to serve as an acolyte in the church. And the terrifying nights of his childhood were interwoven with the sights of the holy city and the fragrance of frankincense. How he suffered through the long hours of incense, song, and prayer. Those endless, unbearable

*Old slides. First of their kind.*

hours, when all his limbs were close to tears and he could not take part in the games and folly of the rest of the boys, neither in the long dormitory rooms at night, nor in the long processionals on holidays. Until one day, on Khatch Küd—the holiday of the discovery of the cross, while in the depths of the Church of the Holy Sepulchre, he slipped away and hid behind one of the columns, remaining there, semi-conscious and forgotten.

And on the following morning, he attached himself to a group of pilgrims, and, hiding behind the back of a portly man, he left for the inn at the American Colony. There, having buried his acolyte's uniform, he hid for two days, and on the third was found and taken in by the good people of the Colony. One more skinny, shivering foundling had been added to their community.

The days and years which he spent with them as a photographer's apprentice were peaceful and lovely. Lovely they were—and now he stands shattered, rummaging in his desk drawer with trembling hands, and I am unable to stop him. I am unable to help him regain his peace of mind, to reinstate him behind the counter.

On the following morning Sahik did not come to the shop.

He joined a swarm of tourists, showed them around the city, and by noon he followed them out the Damascus Gate, where he hopped on a wagon bound for Damascus.

*Old slides. First of their kind.*

And he was never again seen in Jerusalem.

But in the desk drawer in the photographer's studio near the American Colony, there remained, apparently, several slides . . .

And they were destined to multiply and spread like crabgrass, to creep and burst forth from every crack and cleft, and their descendants, the pictures, would rise up to flood me from all directions. Wasn't any place free of them?

*I* was indeed most possessive and jealous of my box of slides, my firstborn, my long gray one, the one and only! I did not care for any other plates or prints. No! After all, mine were one-of-a-kind slides, old ones, and there were no others like them!

"I'll buy the whole box!"

The young, smooth Armenian salesman smiled evasively, raised a fine, long eyebrow, and counted the change into my hand.

At the end of that month, I returned to my home in Boston. Autumn arrived, and I returned to my work and my students at Brandeis.

All through that autumn and the winter that fol-

*Old slides. First of their kind.*

lowed, I nursed the pictures and scenes in my heart anxiously, longingly, hungrily. With the coming of spring, I rented an old-fashioned projector. I bought a large cake, some cookies, a large can of coffee, and some fancy paper napkins. And I invited my students to come to my house on Saturday night for "an evening of slides and coffee."

Some came alone, others in couples or in groups. They were excited and slightly embarrassed. They ate the cake, finished the cookies, and remained standing, pretending to sip the coffee.

"They don't like coffee," I whispered to Edward in despair.

"Don't worry about it," he replied with his wise, kind eyes. "Anyway, we didn't buy Coke or soft drinks, which they do like."

Then, with forced gaiety, I led them into the living room, where they sat down on the floor and the sofa. Edward removed a picture from the wall, secured the projector on its stand, and I began the story: "A Tale of Slides and a Christian Pilgrim to the Holy Land at the End of the Nineteenth Century."

My students, seated on the floor and the sofa, politely and uneasily mumbled in approval.

Did they know, could they guess, how much I loved them? Did they realize that the whole evening was a gift I wanted to give them? Could they sense that I had planned

*Old slides. First of their kind.*

to open a window into my heart for them? A small port-hole? And there I was, forcing upon them a story of love and jealousy for a box.

Oh, my beloved friends.

And we, Edward and I, went on showing the slides and explaining, explaining and showing, until it seemed that they had relaxed, their faces smiling.

They were beginning to ask questions, to joke around. And it was then that my darling student, my gentle pupil, Joseph Sammut my lad, dared to unfold his tale:

During vacation, at his parents' house in Texas, he had climbed up to the attic and lo, among the odds and ends long forgotten in a dusty corner, there lay an old wooden box. And when he lifted the lid, he saw that it was filled with slides, glass slides, thick ones. . . .

Joseph, my son, my gentle pupil, you have just torn me to pieces. The only many-colored coat I have, my one and only, are you about to stain it in blood?

In the silence that fell over the room my students' faces froze.

Strange. Not one of them seemed to rejoice at my calamity. They were silent, glum.

Edward was quiet, too.

What next?

From a distance, I heard my voice attempt a make-shift strategy:

"Let us assume, then, that we have before us a story

*Old slides. First of their kind.*

[ 129 ]

that has no end," my voice babbled. "Let each of you write an end to the story, a final chapter. It will be considered your term paper."

Ha? The cunning one! Should I deal my reader this wise little end as well? Should I leave ten empty pages at the end of the book: To the Reader?

Dear reader, you are hereby invited to fill in these pages any way you please . . .

*E*dward was silent. Why did I glimpse a spark of worry in his eyes?

And Joseph Sammut, my gentle pupil, looked at me with sad brown eyes, and he smiled guiltily. My throat was parched.

"I am athirst, I am a-a-a-thirst, for thy waters, thy waters, Jerusalem."

The sad, forgotten Yemenite tune suddenly rose in me. Did I actually sing? Or was the melody weeping deep inside my heart?

And Joseph Sammut, my gentle lad, whose brown eyes moistened in an embarrassed smile, seemed to offer me a cup of consolation:

*Old slides. First of their kind.*

"In mine," he mumbled, "in my slides, there isn't even one Turkish sentry. Not one."

Edward kept his silence.

Slowly, however, my spirit recovered, and, as if rising from the ruins, it was caught in a strange gaiety and an enthusiasm not my own.

No, a woman like me would never flee. After all, it was not without good reason that I had found that box of sights of the Holy Land and redeemed it from the hands of that drunken scoundrel at the antique shop at the edge of Boston!

And now, was I going to keep it for myself?

Just because fate willed that I, of all the inhabitants of Boston, would find that box, did not mean that I should also take credit for it. After all, it was my calling.

Even before I was born, my name spoke of her—of Jerusalem.

I was seized by a light dizziness. I imagined myself—
Running, rushing,
climbing possessed,
collecting, grabbing,
buying obsessed.
Any wooden box found
I am forced and bound
to buy, to collect,
to conceal and protect.
And so,
from monastery to archive

*Old slides. First of their kind.*

I go
running, rushing, climbing, compelled—
stairs in endless numbers
to attics and chambers,
to towers of bells,
to cellars and cells.
I stumble and stagger
to fairs and to auctions
where treasures lie hidden
in wooden boxes.

And I would buy them all. I would bring them from the East, and I would gather them from the West! I would tell the North: "*Hand over!*" And to Texas: "*Do not hold back!*"

Then, loudly and clearly and with affection, I—the cunning one—turned to Joseph my lad:

"That box you mentioned, Joseph, do you happen to have it with you? No? That's all right. On your next vacation, when you go home to Texas, to your parents, do bring it back with you. You won't forget, now. And you will give it to me, please. On loan?!"

*Old slides. First of their kind.*

# Afterword

"Greta was weaving quiet, slowness, tranquility and yesterday."

Like Arachne, who greatly intrigued her, Ariella was most skilled in the art of weaving. She embroidered her cloth with events and experiences, both collective and personal, of past and present. Her narrative is rooted in the Bible and Midrash; her lyrical prose spans the breadth of the Hebrew language from its ancient Semitic origins, through the Mishnah, the Talmud, the Piyyutim, medieval verse, and modern poetry. The classics of world literature have also left their mark on her writing. Her storytelling possesses an incantatory power that calls upon the deepest sensibilities of her readers, compelling them to return for more.

The characters in *Jerusalem Plays Hide and Seek* mirror various aspects of Ariella's singular personality. Many of the events are autobiographical. The "story of love and jealousy for a box" is clearly an offering. Ariella has shared with her readers wisdom and joy, agony and folly, and, above all, an acute and profound awareness of historical connectedness in all its tragic and transcendent implications.

Ariella was interviewed on Israeli radio and television on several occasions, but only once was a talk with her published. It appeared in *Bitzaron, A Quarterly Review of Hebrew Letters,* Winter–Spring 1984. Answering the questions posed by her interviewer, the Israeli poet Avner Trainin, Ariella shed light on some of the subtleties in her fiction; on the juxtaposition of the fantastic and the real. Yet even repeated readings do not dissolve the aura of ambiguity that marks the interview. Like this book, it seems to be touched by the mythical. When Trainin asked her about the recurrent use of repetitions, shadows, reflections, and mirror images in her writing, she replied:

"*From an artistic point of view, whatever we try to do seems like a shadow, a reflection, as it were, of something that has already been done. I want the readers to join me in this feeling from the start, and therefore it appears as if I am embroidering right before their eyes; including them in this sense of shadows. [Moreover,] whatever happens on the level of the narrator happens later to one of the characters, or vice versa.*"

"*You mean, first the reflection and then the thing itself?*"

"*Yes. That is, on the level of the embroidery. But then there seems to be another level. . . . It is a matter of being a part of a certain destiny, a fate. The fate of the Jewish people has generally been a matter of reflections. Whatever happened would happen again, as if mirrored, as if subjected to a law of repetition, where things would go on revolving, either back and forth, or in a circular motion. [The direction] isn't quite clear.*"

At some point in this story, there looms a sense of inherent helplessness, a fate of timeless visions and omnipotent decrees:

> On that Yom Kippur the synagogue at Brandeis University was filled to capacity. It was a lovely Tishrei day. A beautiful autumn day. . . . And through the windows, the green hills of Boston were rising.
>
> What had come over them . . . Were they about to burst? A portentous day.
>
> And by noon the bad news had already been rolling like a storm. . . . My anguish, my anguish! For I heard the sound of the shofar, the alarm of war. And then the radio and television sets began carrying the horror. . . . What was happening? Had the Lord risen up as on Mount Perazim to do His deed? Strange was His deed! Had He really planned to gather all the multitude of nations that fight against Ariel?

The solemn tone of the narrative is achieved through artful and allusive use of language and through repetitions. The pattern of repetition appears, at first, to follow a literary convention but then becomes the axis on which the characters and events rotate. It is transformed into a rhythm that wells up on its own—like Luna Meyuhas's laughter, which echoes that of Efrem son of Ingmar. The repetitive structure of her books, Ariella told Trainin:

> *"began as a literary, stylistic device. This is how it began in* Jerusalem. *But then I saw that it was a part of the whole thing, and that I could hardly control it. . . . Even if it began*

*as a device, it was, in fact, the thing itself, and I had no control over it. The outer repetitions express the inner happenings—the reflections game."*

Ariella's contributions to scholarly publications are focused on literary approaches to biblical topics as well as biblical patterns in modern literature. Trainin asked her about the relationship between her research and her literary activity.

*"When I work on an obscure problem [in biblical research], I believe that I follow the accepted norms of academic research. That is, up to a certain point. Up to the point when the problem becomes clear, and a picture suddenly unfolds before me. An interpretation of a picture, or a picture of the interpretation. And suddenly I get very excited. The moment the question has been resolved, I get very excited and feel a strong urge to leave it as a research topic . . . what has now become legitimate research material in the eyes of the academicians suddenly erupts from me, imploring me to do with it something else."*

After she found the box of slides in the antique shop in Boston, Ariella tried, together with her husband, Edward Goldberg, to trace its origins. They had been gathering fragments of information when she suddenly realized that the treasure lay buried elsewhere, and she stopped. She began to spin a tapestry of dazzling colors, set against the background of Jerusalem between the centuries. She wove together the historic, the fantastic and the real, with words marked by an archaic flavor, playing a subtle game of hide and seek.

"*Was I ever permitted to enter the Holy of Holies? To touch the twelve precious stones on the breastplate of Aaron, the high priest? But when I recall their names, or when I simply hold a pen in my hand, it seems as if I have just buried both my hands in a box full of pearls and gone wild. I play with the words, and they string themselves, and they sparkle, no less than the glass beads I used to find on the paths of my childhood. . . . Ruby, topaz, agate . . .*"

Ariella was my best friend. From the paths of our childhood in Beit Oved to that gray winter day in Boston, in 1985, when she said, "Nellichka, the show is over." Look, Ariellinka, take a look, Queen of Jerusalem. See how it goes on: "An autumn day in Boston lost its mind and masqueraded as spring. . . ."

Nelly Segal